BRANDED BY THE PINK TRIANGLE

Branded by the Pink Triangle

KEN SETTERINGTON

Second Story Press

Library and Archives Canada Cataloguing in Publication

Setterington, Ken
Branded by the pink triangle / Ken Setterington.

Includes index.
Issued also in an electronic format.
ISBN 978-1-926920-96-2

1. Gays—Nazi persecution—Juvenile literature. 2. World War, 1939–1945—Atrocities—Juvenile literature. 3. World War, 1939–1945—Concentration camp—Juvenile literature. I. Title.

D804.5.G38S48 2013 j940.53'1808664 C2012-908181-7

Third Printing 2014

Edited by: Malcolm Lester, Jonathan Schmidt, Carolyn Jackson
Copyedited by: Kathryn White
Designed by: Melissa Kaita

Printed and bound in Canada

Second Story Press gratefully acknowledges the support of the Ontario Arts Council and the Canada Council for the Arts for our publishing program. We acknowledge the financial support of the Government of Canada through the Canada Book Fund.

Published by
SECOND STORY PRESS
20 Maud Street, Suite 401
Toronto, ON M5V 2M5
www.secondstorypress.ca

This book is dedicated to the memory of the men who suffered at the hands of the Nazis simply because they were gay, and to those in countries around the world who still suffer because they are gay.

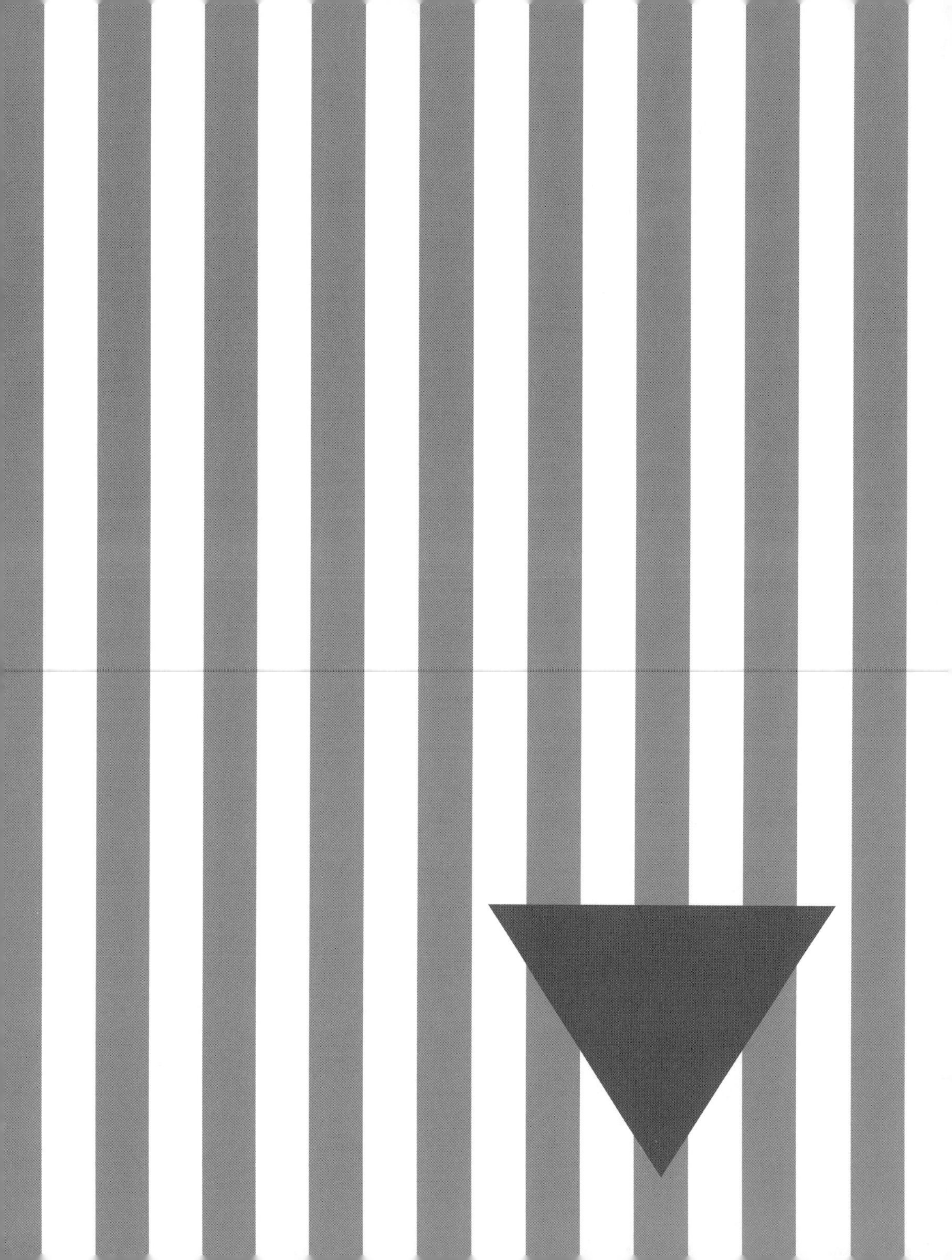

Contents

PREFACE		1
CHAPTER 1	Berlin – Homosexual Capital of Europe	3
CHAPTER 2	The Rise of the Nazis	9
CHAPTER 3	The Gay Life Is Over	25
CHAPTER 4	The Master Race – The Nazi Plan to Rid Germany of the Inferior	37
CHAPTER 5	Death through Work – Imprisonment in the Concentration Camps	55
CHAPTER 6	Nazis in Occupied Territories	75
CHAPTER 7	Jewish Homosexuals	81
CHAPTER 8	Aftermath	91
CHAPTER 9	Recognition at Last	97
CHAPTER 10	The Survivors	103
CONCLUSION	It Gets Better	113
AFTERWORD		119
ACKNOWLEDGMENTS		121
APPENDIX	Timeline	123
BIBLIOGRAPHY		133
NOTES		137
INDEX		143
PHOTO CREDITS		153

Preface

On a cold, snowy day in 1944, a man in the regulation prison uniform of Nazi Germany's notorious Auschwitz concentration camp approached the huge stinking pit that served as a latrine in the prison yard. He had watched from a distance as a trainload of Jewish women and girls were herded into the camp. They had been showered in boiling hot water and now – naked, wet, and shivering – they were forced to stand outside in the snow to dry off before being sent to the primitive latrines. He had seen a young girl awkwardly trying to crouch on narrow planks over the hole and had watched as a guard pushed her with a stick, unbalancing her and sending her into the pit of stinking waste. The prisoner reached the pit and looked down as the other prisoners were marched off to their barracks. There sat the girl, naked, embarrassed, and covered in excrement.

Ashamed and terrified, sixteen-year-old Kitty Fischer looked up and saw the prisoner. There was something different about him. Jewish prisoners were issued shirts with yellow stars sewn on the front. This man had a pink triangle on his. While he helped Kitty out of the filth she asked the man about his pink triangle. He told her why he had to wear it and after they found her sister, he promised he would return.

A short time later the pink triangle man appeared with a jacket potato for each of the girls to eat. In the weeks that followed, he returned repeatedly with smuggled potatoes. He was risking his own life to help the girls survive. Kitty vowed that she would never forget the humanity and kindness of their protector.

Decades later, she found a way to make sure the world would finally understand the persecution and suffering of the thousands like him – homosexuals who were branded by the pink triangle.

CHAPTER 1

Berlin – Homosexual Capital of Europe

In the early years of the twentieth century, life was extremely difficult for gay men and women. In cities that now celebrate gay pride, homosexuals[1] were actively persecuted. Laws prohibited sex between men. As a result, most homosexuals were forced to lead secret lives and had to establish their own underground networks.

Still, there were exceptions – and Berlin was an exceptional city.

Life for homosexuals in Germany was much easier than it was in the rest of Europe, or indeed in the rest of the world. The German laws that prohibited sex between men were seldom enforced, and homosexual culture thrived. Berlin was recognized as its capital.

Several German publications catered to gay men and women: *Menschenrecht* (Human Rights), *Die Insel* (The Island), and *Der Eigene*

For young homosexual couples such as this one, life in Berlin in the early 1900s was free and easy.

(His Own Self) for men, and *Ledige Frauen* (Single Women), *Frauenliebe* (Women's Love), and *Die Freundin* (The Girlfriend) for lesbians.

Many clubs and bars, restaurants, and popular dance clubs, all within Berlin's gay section, drew patrons who preferred to be intimate with members of their own sex. Sometimes in these settings it was hard to tell who was a man and who was a woman.

Menschenrecht (Human Rights) was just one of the many newspapers, magazines, and journals published specifically for the homosexual reader.

People from around the world traveled to Berlin to enjoy the freedom of this exciting atmosphere. A survivor of the period remembered the Schwanenburg, a popular club he frequented.

> It was a dance club, a normal bar, but on certain days it was rented by homosexuals. Then there was much joy.... There was homosexual dancing and once in a while just to get the queens going,

ABOVE: The gay district of Berlin was home to many bars, restaurants, and nightclubs. Often it was hard to tell the sex of patrons as their dress, hairstyles, and makeup often defied the norm.

RIGHT: Club Violetta appealed to lesbians. Homosexuals from around the world came to Berlin to experience the gay lifestyle.

Damenklub Violetta

im Jägerhof-Kasino, Hasenheide 52-53

Mittwoch (Bußtag), den 21. November

ab 5 Uhr **Kaffeekränzchen**

mit Vortragsabend und Klubbesprechungen bis 1 Uhr

Eintritt frei f. M.

Sonnabend, den 24. November

Italienische Nacht mit intimer Lampionbeleuchtung

Anfang abends 8 Uhr .˙ Ende 3 Uhr .˙ Eintritt frei f. M.

Stimmungs-Jazz-Trio mit dem bekannten Millionenmax

Sonntag (Totensonntag), den 25. November

Ab 5 Uhr **Kaffeekränzchen**

mit Vortragsabend und Vereinsbesprechungen. Eintritt frei f. M.

Es ladet alle liebenDamen hierzu herzlichst ein LOTTE HAHM

Untergrundbahn: Station Hasenheide (vorm Hause). Omnibus: 4, 29.

Straßenbahn: 3, 5, 15, 58, 115.

> someone would shout, "The police are coming!" Everyone would hike up their skirts and run. But the police never really came.... It is hard to imagine how wild it was in Berlin...men danced with men, women danced with women. In Berlin, those were the golden years. [2]

In 1918, the first international gay-themed film, *Anders als die Andern* (Different from the Others), was made in Germany. Produced to educate the public about homosexuality, it was co-written by Dr. Magnus Hirschfeld, a researcher in human sexuality who also appeared in the film.

The first gay film *Anders als die Andern* (Different from the Others) was written and produced in Germany in 1918.

The British writer Christopher Isherwood left England to live in Berlin in the 1920s because it was a much more exciting place to live as a gay man than anywhere else in the world. Many years later, when he was famous, he wrote of his Berlin experiences in the 1976 book *Christopher and His Kind.* But the book that made him so famous, *Goodbye to Berlin,* he had written decades earlier; it included descriptions of the characters, energy, and decadence he found in the city. Isherwood wrote about the notorious Kit Kat Club, immortalizing it for future generations. *Goodbye to Berlin* was produced as a play, *I Am a Camera,* and then later made into the award-winning Broadway musical and film *Cabaret.*

For many gay men and women in Berlin, life was indeed a cabaret during the 1920s and early 1930s. But as Isherwood's book forecast, there was a very dark cloud looming on the horizon.

CHAPTER 2

The Rise of the Nazis

The First World War (1914 – 1918) left Germany virtually bankrupt and suffering in its defeat. Poverty and unemployment became part of daily life. As a condition of surrender, Germany had been forced to sign the Treaty of Versailles, accepting responsibility for starting the war and agreeing to pay reparations of 132 billion Reichsmarks (more than US$400 billion today) to help cover the damages from the war. When the Great Depression hit in 1929, the effect on Germany was catastrophic. Poverty increased. Unemployment increased. Inflation increased. Desperation increased. By 1933, unemployment had reached six million – more than 30 percent, an unprecedented level. People wanted jobs and a way out of the miserable lives they were living. They needed something – or someone – to believe in.

Adolf Hitler and his Nazi Party provided hope of a prosperous future. He promised those who flocked to hear him that he would defy the Treaty of Versailles, rebuild the military, and unite Germany, including all the Germans in Poland, Czechoslovakia, and Austria.

He claimed that Germany's defeat in 1918 could have been prevented had it not been for the actions of traitorous Jews. The Jew was Germany's natural enemy. "In standing guard against the Jew, I am defending the handiwork of the Lord," Hitler wrote. (1)

For desperate citizens who wanted to believe in the future, Hitler and the Nazi Party made them feel that pride in being German was once again possible. The Nazi Party would rescue Germany from the shame of defeat and provide Aryan Germans with a glorious future.

▼

When the Nazi Party began its persecution of homosexuals, it did not need to create new laws to prohibit homosexual behavior. As noted, a law against homosexuality already existed. All the Nazis had to do was enforce it.

The law that prohibited sex between men was called Paragraph 175. It dated back to 1871, when the King of Prussia united various kingdoms into one German state with a new constitution and a set of laws. Paragraph 175 stated, "A man who commits indecency with another man, or allows himself to be misused indecently, will be punished with prison."(2)

In the years before the rise of the Nazis, there might have been 1,000 arrests each year under this law, but few of the arrests ever resulted in a prison sentence. Most "offenders" were fined, warned about their "deviant" behavior, and released. In fact, so lax had enforcement been over the years that activists were working to abolish Paragraph 175 altogether.

They believed that homosexuality was as natural as heterosexuality, and they tried to reform both the law and the attitudes of society. Dr. Magnus Hirschfeld was the most prominent of these activists, and he also campaigned for the rights of women, including abortion rights.

A 1907 political cartoon depicting sex-researcher Dr. Magnus Hirschfeld drumming up support for the abolition of the German penal code's Paragraph 175, which criminalized homosexuality. The banner reads, "Away with Paragraph 175!" The caption reads, "The foremost champion of the third sex!"

Hirschfeld was born in 1868 into a German Jewish family. He studied medicine, became a doctor, and practiced as a physician for a number of

years, but soon found his passion lay in being an outspoken advocate for the rights of homosexuals.

His advocacy and research into human sexuality became his life's work. He believed that only through the scientific examination of homosexuality would society understand that it was not to be feared or punished. In 1897, Hirschfeld founded the Scientific-Humanitarian Committee and gathered more than 5,000 signatures on a petition from prominent citizens to overturn Paragraph 175. The signatories included some of the most influential Germans of the time, including scientist Albert Einstein, writers Hermann Hesse and Thomas Mann, poet Rainer Maria Rilke, and philosopher Martin Buber. The petition was not successful, but Dr. Hirschfeld continued his work and by 1919 had founded the Institute for Sexual Research. The Institute became internationally famous for its extensive library and its original and groundbreaking scientific research, attracting scientists from around the world.

Dr. Hirschfeld's international influence was enhanced when he organized the First Congress for Sexual Reform in Berlin in 1921. This congress was followed by conferences in Copenhagen, London, Vienna, and Brno during the 1920s. But while the doctor was busy with his research, conditions in Germany were worsening, providing fertile ground for the growth of the Nazi Party.

Although Magnus Hirschfeld may have convinced German intellectuals that Paragraph 175 needed to be abolished, and was building

LEFT: A researcher studies photographs in the library at the Institute for Sexual Research in Berlin.

support to strike it down, at the same time the rising power of the Nazis indicated that there was much to fear. The Nazis believed that Hirschfeld was a homosexual himself, who simply wanted homosexuality to thrive. They argued that this would mean fewer German babies and hence a lower birth rate, which would ultimately lead to a weaker Germany. Hirschfeld was also a Jew, and the opinions of Jews were not to be given any consideration in Hitler's Germany. In the Party's official newspaper it was recorded that "among the many evil instincts that characterize the Jewish race, one that is especially pernicious has to do with sexual relationships between siblings, men and animals, and men and men.... These efforts are nothing but vulgar, perverted crimes and we will punish them by banishment or hanging." (3)

Some members of the Nazi Party also were advocating the inclusion of lesbians in the restrictive legislation. The Nazis had outlined their position on homosexuality in 1928, when responding to queries about Paragraph 175:

> It is not necessary that you and I live, but it is necessary that German people live. And it can only live if it can fight, life means fighting. And it can only fight if it maintains its masculinity. It can only maintain its masculinity if it exercises discipline, especially in matters of love. Free love and deviance are undisciplined. Therefore, we reject you, as we reject anything that hurts our nation. Anyone who thinks of homosexual love is our enemy. We reject anything which emasculates our people and makes it a plaything for our enemies, for

> we know that life is a fight, and it is madness to think that men will ever embrace fraternally. Natural history teaches us the opposite. Might makes right. The strong will always win over the weak. Let us see to it that we once again become the strong! But this we can achieve only in one way – the German people must once again learn how to exercise discipline. We therefore reject any form of lewdness, especially homosexuality, because it robs us of our last chance to free our people from the bondage which now enslaves it. (4)

For homosexuals the future was bleak. The Nazi Party had made its ideology clear. The Party platform was based on rebuilding Germany through strong "law and order" policies, traditional values, and "racial purity." This "pure" race certainly did not include Jews or any other persons deemed undesirable by the Nazis – and homosexuals were definitely undesirable.

To the general public, rights for homosexuals were not a burning issue. The need for jobs and money was far more important.

In July of 1932, the Nazi Party won the most seats in the German parliament, though not a majority. Hitler could now form a government in coalition with others. Eventually, the parties of the center and right agreed to accept Hitler as leader, and in January 1933, he was named Chancellor of Germany.

The next month, homosexual rights organizations were banned. The Nazis moved quickly to suppress any objectors to the new regime. Enemies of the state were rounded up in raids on homes and businesses. In an effort to ease the burden on the prison system, Heinrich Himmler, head of the SS (*Schutzstaffel*), the elite protection guard of the Nazi state, set up the first concentration camp at Dachau. It opened shortly after Hitler was appointed Chancellor. Dachau was the first of many camps used as prisons for the enemies of the Nazis and the "inferiors" – Jews, Roma and Sinti (commonly referred to at the time as Gypsies), homosexuals, and

Good times at the popular Eldorado nightclub ended in 1933 when the Nazis closed it down.

Jehovah's Witnesses. Among the first prisoners in Dachau were men who had worked in homosexual rights organizations in Berlin.

Attacks against homosexuals began in earnest. In February 1933, the gay and lesbian bars were closed, and all publications for homosexuals were banned. The famous Berlin club Eldorado was shut down in early March.

On May 6, 1933, the Nazis stormed Hirschfeld's Institute for Sexual Research, smashing all they could. A few days later, a massive book burning was organized that destroyed more than twelve thousand books as well as Dr. Hirschfeld's important collection of photographs.

Police maintained watch after the closure of Eldorado.
The club was quickly plastered with pro-Nazi election posters.

Fortunately, Dr. Hirschfeld was out of the country on a speaking engagement. He never returned to Germany, dying in France in 1935. His gravestone is engraved with his Latin motto, *Per Scientiam ad Justitiam* (Through Science to Justice).

Homosexuals hoped that these incidents were just a show of power, and that the pressure on them would ease in a few months. It was widely known that one of Hitler's most influential deputies, Ernst Röhm, was a homosexual, and this may have encouraged the belief that the attacks

The Nazis organized the burning of thousands of "un-German" books and Dr. Hirschfield's collection of photographs at Berlin' s Opernplatz a few days after storming his research institute.

would be short lived. As one survivor recounted, "Röhm was a homosexual man; everyone knew it. The homosexual people were quite sure that nothing would happen because one of the government men was like them." (5)

They soon learned how wrong they were.

▼

Many considered Ernst Röhm the second-most powerful man in Germany. Röhm first met Adolf Hitler in 1919 and quickly became

Ernst Röhm (center), seen here in his SA uniform, had been friends with Adolf Hitler since 1919, despite the fact that Röhm was a homosexual.

Hitler's most trusted friend. Röhm's organizational skills and his ability to gain respect from all sorts of men made him a great asset to Hitler, who was willing to overlook Röhm's homosexuality – until it stood in the way of his own power.

In the early 1920s, while the Nazi Party was being solidified, Hitler had formed his own paramilitary group known as the SA (*Sturmabteilungen*, literally Storm Section). Its members were easily identified by their uniforms of gray jackets, brown shirts, knee breeches, and swastika armbands. The men were mostly ex-soldiers and beer-hall

This anti-Nazi cartoon entitled "Röhm inspects the SA parade," was published in the *Red Pepper*, the satirical newspaper of the German communist party.

brawlers – a rough band known as the Storm Troopers or Brownshirts. They were given the task of disrupting the meetings of opposing political parties and of protecting Hitler from revenge attacks. Ernst Röhm became the first leader of the SA, and Hitler relied on his friend to help build the SA and support for the Nazi Party.

Within the Party, there were concerns raised about Röhm's homosexuality, but Hitler stood by Röhm, stating, "[The SA] is not an institution for the moral education of genteel young ladies, but a formation of seasoned fighters.... His private life cannot be an object of scrutiny unless it conflicts with basic principles of National Socialist ideology." (6)

By the early 1930s, the SA had ballooned to more than three million men and had helped secure Hitler's power. When Hitler became Chancellor, he needed to solidify his power with new supporters – including the the *Reichswehr*, the traditional German army. The army was filled with "old generals" and men of position, and not at all with the rough sort of bullies who filled the ranks of the SA. Röhm wanted the much smaller Reichswehr to become part of the SA under his command, but the traditional army men did not consider Röhm a suitable choice for the head of the army. One general said, "Re-armament is too serious and militarily important to be left to hoodlums and homosexuals like Captain Röhm." (7)

It was clear to Hitler that the army elite would never agree to serve under Röhm's command, so he made a pact with the army's top brass that he himself would be their leader, and that Röhm and his SA would lose power. Röhm was unaware of these plans until early 1934 when Hitler announced that the army was to be the single legitimate German military force. Röhm was furious, but could do little.

While Hitler was reducing Röhm's influence, Heinrich Himmler (head of the SS), Reinhard Heydrich (head of Nazi intelligence), and Hermann Göring (head of the *Luftwaffe*, or Air Force) were anxious to gain more control within the Nazi Party. They realized that the best way to do this was to eliminate Röhm completely. They created documents that implicated Röhm in a plot to stage a coup within the Nazi Party.

That was all the evidence Hitler needed.

On June 4, he had a meeting with Röhm and attempted to reason with him. The meeting lasted for five hours and it was to be their last. Röhm and Hitler had been friends, but he was no longer useful.

Within days, plans were in place for "Operation Hummingbird." Röhm was told that Hitler would meet with him and the SA leadership on July 1. Instead, on June 29, 1934, Hitler, accompanied by his personal SS guards, arrested Röhm. During the next twenty-four hours unsuspecting senior Storm Trooper officers were arrested as they made their way to the "meeting." Many were shot immediately, but Röhm was held prisoner while Hitler decided what to do with him.

On July 1, an SS officer entered Röhm's prison cell and handed him a revolver. Röhm is supposed to have said, "Let Adolf do it himself." Röhm was executed by two SS hit men, his body and those of the other executed SA men hauled away in a butcher's tin-lined truck so that their murders could be kept secret.

The elimination of the SA elite was not revealed until July 13 when Hitler spoke of the purge, calling it the "Night of the Long Knives." He claimed that sixty-one SA members had been executed, thirteen had been shot while resisting arrest, and three others had committed suicide. Other sources state that as many as 400 died during those few days. When discussing the murder of these men, Hitler proclaimed, "If anyone reproaches me and asks why I did not resort to the regular courts of justice, then all I can say is this: In this hour I was responsible for the fate of the German people. I became the supreme judge of the German nation."(8) Hitler also referred specifically to the homosexuality of Röhm and some other men in the SA, ensuring that the public understood he had rid the SA of these deviants.

CHAPTER 3

The Gay Life Is Over

The Night of the Long Knives was a huge triumph for Hitler. It established him as above the law and as the supreme judge for the German people. The purge of the SA was the first great show of violence under Nazi rule. It would not be the last. Hitler had taken a giant step closer to creating his Master Race. There was no place for homosexuality within the Master Race.

Röhm had been a very public figure in Germany, and his murder delivered a strong message. Now that the Party had been cleansed, the targets became any men who preferred to have sex with other men. One such man was Rudolf Brazda.

Born in Brossen, Germany, in 1913, Rudolf was the eighth child of a miner and his wife. He knew from an early age that he was more interested in boys than girls. Growing up, he made it clear that he did not plan to follow in his father's footsteps to work in the mines; instead he hoped to work in the men's fashion industry. But jobs were scarce, and Rudolf needed to work, so he ended up training as a roofer. As a teenager during the era of relaxed attitudes toward homosexuals, Rudolf's life was relatively easy. He was twenty years old when he met his lover, Werner, in 1933. The two lived together, boarding in the home of a woman who was a Jehovah's Witness. Even though their relationship was not condoned by her religion, she allowed the young men to live there. Their relationship was accepted, and Rudolf and Werner even held a ceremony to acknowledge their commitment to each other, with Rudolf's mother and siblings in attendance.

Like all homosexuals, Rudolf was aware of Paragraph 175, but he and most other homosexuals knew that usually they would be left alone if they were discreet and were not seeking relationships with young boys. However, as all homosexuals in Germany were to discover, this world was changing more rapidly than they could imagine.

Rudolf had his first encounter with German authorities when he was found in the Café New York, a well-known gay haunt in Leipzig. Nazi storm troopers dragged everyone out by their hair. Rudolf was not arrested, but the brutality of the event made him aware that gathering in public was not going to be tolerated any longer. In 1936, Werner enlisted in the military to do his compulsory service. Rudolf took a position in a Leipzig hotel. A year later, when the Nazis increased their efforts to find and prosecute homosexuals, Rudolf was arrested as a suspected homosexual and charged with "unnatural lewdness." The arrest came after the police had investigated some of his friends. He was sentenced to six months in prison.

Meanwhile, even though Werner was in the military, he, too, was arrested and sentenced, but his trial was in another city. The two men, who had committed themselves to each other, were unable to maintain any contact. Rudolf never saw Werner again.

Rudolf served his six months and upon release was expelled from Germany. Because his parents had originally been from Czechoslovakia, he was now considered a non-German with a criminal record – someone deemed unsuitable for Germany. Given no choice, he left Germany and settled in Carlsbad, in what is now the Czech Republic, even though he spoke no Czech. With his training as a roofer, Rudolf was able to find work, but his freedom was short lived. Germany invaded Czechoslovakia in 1938.

Fear dominated life for homosexuals. When interviewed years later, Rudolf said, "We gays were hunted like animals." (1) Once again he was arrested after some of his acquaintances were interrogated and his past arrest was revealed. And once again he was imprisoned. At the end of his fifteen-month sentence, Rudolf was not released but rather put into *Schutzhaft,* or "protective custody." Three months later, on August 8, 1942, he was deported to Buchenwald concentration camp, prisoner number 7952.

At the camp, he and the other arrivals were herded into a room with a pool in it. The men had to strip and enter the pool, which was filled with disinfectant. When an SS officer saw that Rudolf was wearing a gold chain and cross, he ripped it off and pushed Rudolf's head into the disinfectant. Choking and with his eyes burning, Rudolf was given his prison uniform along with a large pink triangle to be sewn on the left breast. This would identify him as a "fag" to all the other prisoners. Rudolf remarked years later, "It was

Roll call was a twice-daily ordeal of several hours for prisoners at Buchenwald concentration camp. Homosexual prisoners were identified by pink triangle badges and identification numbers.

so ridiculous – the color pink…of course we were laughed at. Of course, the color pink!" (2)

Close to a quarter of a million people were incarcerated at Buchenwald during the years from 1938 to 1945. Rudolf Brazda was one of 650 men who were sent there because of Paragraph 175. Homosexual prisoners were assigned to grueling and dangerous work in the stone quarry, an assignment that few could survive. Rudolf remembered one young gay man who gouged out his eyes so that he would be sent to the infirmary instead of the quarry, even though he knew that it wasn't uncommon for lethal injections to be given to sick or handicapped prisoners in the infirmary. For him, a lethal injection must have seemed better than what was waiting for him at the quarry.

Rudolf started working there himself, and his youth and good looks soon brought him the attention of a *kapo.* (Though technically a prisoner, a kapo had some authority in the camp and many additional privileges.) Rudolf's kapo assigned him to a less demanding detachment where he could work as a roofer. He saved Rudolf's life on several occasions. Once, when answering a question from an SS officer, Rudolf gave the wrong answer. The officer struck him in anger, knocking out three of his teeth and sentencing him to death the following day. The kapo intervened, claiming that Brazda, as a roofer, was an important worker, and so the death penalty was never enforced.

Rudolf Brazda attributed his survival in the camp where so many other pink triangles died to the fact that he was a good age, and that he had useful skills. Had he gotten his wish years before and found a job in the fashion industry instead of roofing, he no doubt would have perished.

In March 1945, when it became clear that the war was coming to an end, the Nazis evacuated Buchenwald, and prisoners were forced on a death march to camps deeper inside German territory. During the march thousands died from exhaustion or were shot by the SS. Once again Rudolf was fortunate to have captured the affection of a kapo who was in charge of the stables. He hid Rudolf in a shed with the pigs. He stayed hidden for fourteen days, living on food smuggled to him by the kapo. Rudolf Brazda was liberated by the Americans when they arrived at the camp on April 11, 1945.

▼

Fear of arrest made men try to hide their homosexuality. But there really was no sure way to do so. Some homosexual men joined the army, hoping that they would be safe from arrest. Others married, hoping to make people believe that they were heterosexual. Lesbians proved to be helpful to some, marrying homosexual men to prevent their being arrested. While lesbians were not targeted in the same manner as homosexual men, the collective lesbian lifestyle that had flourished in Berlin was over.

Lesbians were no longer flaunting their lifestyle, and some were marrying to avoid societal pressures. The Nazis had launched a massive propaganda campaign in support of marriage, and lesbians were aware of possible backlash if they remained single. One woman recalls the following:

My second girlfriend, Else, married Fritz, a homosexual secondary school teacher, in 1937. He was once at a bar with a friend – not in the back where people were dancing, they were sitting in the bar in front. There was a raid. He was able to talk his way out of it saying they just wanted to have a beer and went into the bar by chance. The men in the back were all taken away, but the two of them were able to go home. At the school where he taught, they told him he should get married since he was already forty. He got to know my girlfriend, though by then we weren't together anymore. Else didn't want her family to find out about her, so they just got married. She had a girlfriend and he had boyfriends. [3]

Nazis viewed women first and foremost as the producers of children. They were to be involved in "*Kinder, Küche, Kirche*" (children, kitchen, and church). Lesbians were not considered harmful to the regime, so they were not targeted in the same manner as male homosexuals. Small numbers of lesbians were arrested and suffered in concentration camps, but they were most often labeled as anti-social members of society.

For men, the consequences of being suspected of homosexuality could be deadly. Even men from powerful, well-connected families had difficulty avoiding arrest if they were homosexual. One such young man was Peter Flinsch, who hoped to hide his sexuality while in the military.

Peter Flinsch grew up in Leipzig in a luxurious home and in a family that was culturally refined. His father's family fortune came from paper and printing businesses, and his mother's from banking and steel interests. Peter's parents divorced when he was only three, and he was raised by his mother and her family.

Peter Flinsch

His maternal grandfather had a major collection of art that included a work by Rembrandt. Peter's early love of art was actively encouraged – he was even allowed to draw on the walls of his nursery. When he was thirteen, he was sent off to continue his artistic education at a prestigious boarding school, chosen by Flinsch's family because it promised a well-rounded education with an emphasis on the development of the full personality. Peter could focus on the study of art as part of his education. His classmates included many well-connected young men, the sons of both the military and industrial elites. His roommate was the Prince of Hanover. Peter looked like the ideal Aryan male: his blond, handsome looks could have made him a poster boy for the Hitler Youth. And of course, like all the other boys in the school, Peter *was* a member of the Hitler Youth.

While Peter's school may have provided a well-rounded education, little was taught about sex except for a lecture on the evils of masturbation. The lecturer stressed the need to "save your strength for a good German girl." Flinsch remembered many passionate friendships that were established in the single-sex school, and when the students masturbated, he said, they thought, "What the hell, we're not going to save it for a good German girl." [4]

After graduation, Flinsch wanted to continue his studies as an artist, but his family doubted that an artist's career would bring financial security. In response, Peter decided to study the more reliable and lucrative field of architecture. But like all young German men, he was faced with a two-year commitment for military service. The question was whether he should study first and then enlist or get his obligatory service out of the way and then complete his studies. Peter decided to enlist first so that his university education would not be interrupted. He also knew that by enlisting, he would be able to join the service of his choice. His mother considered the Luftwaffe the safest place for him, and, through her connections, he was accepted into an anti-aircraft unit.

Peter had known since his late teens that he was homosexual. "Of course I knew.... I found out pretty much after I turned eighteen that my preference was for men." [5] But serving in the Luftwaffe meant his options for exploring his sexuality were limited. He was well aware that the punishment for homosexuality was severe, and, no doubt like other homosexuals in the military, he limited his contact with other like-minded men.

In December 1942, Peter had just completed his officer training, and was one week away from receiving his commission, when he was denounced as a homosexual. At a Christmas party in Berlin, he had become slightly drunk and had shared a single boozy kiss with a subordinate. Peter later said, "It was friendly, but it was at the wrong time, in the wrong place. My whole life was changed by that." (6)

A disgruntled sergeant serving under Flinsch witnessed the kiss and blackmailed the subordinate into stating that Flinsch had propositioned him. Peter was quickly arrested. When his case came to trial, he admitted to having homosexual feelings. This was enough for the military court to find him guilty under Paragraph 175. Because he was in the Luftwaffe, he was not treated as harshly as others. His sentence was three months in prison, to be followed by service in a *Strafkompanie,* a work unit for criminals.

Peter's life as a pampered, wealthy young man was over. He served three months in a Nazi prison, where life was degrading. He had to announce twice a day to his fellow prisoners that he was a homosexual. The daily humiliation and feelings of disgrace both for himself and his family were almost unbearable. He considered suicide and might have killed himself had his mother not managed to visit and tell him, "You're my son. I love you whatever happens." (7) Her encouragement gave him the strength to carry on.

Peter Flinsch's mother had extremely useful connections. She was friends with the wife of a high Nazi official in Berlin, who helped get Peter's sentence revised. A psychiatrist was sent to visit Peter and make the declaration that he was not a homosexual, but rather a man who had made a youthful mistake. This allowed Peter to leave prison at the end of his term and serve as a regular soldier at the front. But he was not allowed to return to the Luftwaffe. Even with strong connections, a conviction under Paragraph 175 was not to be dismissed.

In March 1945, just before the end of the war, Peter was stationed in Hungary and was wounded in his arm and down his side by shrapnel. The train on which he was sent back to Germany was bombarded by artillery, but he managed to escape and was allowed to return to his family.

It had been more than two years since that fateful kiss.

CHAPTER 4

The Master Race – The Nazi Plan to Rid Germany of the Inferior

The persecution of homosexuals was just a small part of Hitler's plan to strengthen the Aryan race. Hitler's regime proclaimed that the "Aryan" or "Nordic" race was biologically superior to all others. Jews, along with the Roma and Sinti, were inferior or subhuman and needed to be eliminated; Poles and other Slavic peoples were also inferior, but were useful as forced labor. The regime found scientists who were willing to support the ideas of racial purity and the biological superiority of Germans. Strict laws were passed ensuring that Jews could not marry Aryans. The Aryan race had to be strengthened by eliminating any weakness.

Men, women, and children who were deemed hereditarily "less valuable" were targeted by the Nazis. It was argued that people with mental or physical disabilities were a burden on society and needed to be removed. The first programs of "mercy killings" began in 1939 with young children under the age of three. All children with severe birth defects had to be registered. Doctors evaluated each case and chose the children to be murdered. After 1939, Hitler authorized the expansion of the killing program from children to adults. It was called Operation T – from the address of the program's headquarters on the Tiergartenstrasse in Berlin. Institutionalized adult patients were immediately targeted. People who were unable to work were vulnerable. More than 70,000 men and women were killed during the first two years of the program, many by lethal gas.

Homosexuals, of course, posed a threat to the building of the new master race. The master race needed strong Aryan men and women who were able to work and reproduce. Anyone who did not fit this mold would be eliminated.

In appearance, some gay German men with tall, blond, good looks may have been perfect examples of Aryan superiority, but if those men preferred having sex with other men, then it was clear that they would not be reproducing. New German babies were the priority, and men who didn't reproduce were a drain on the regime. The Nazis feared that gays would recruit other men to a homosexual lifestyle, thus reducing the number of eligible men for reproduction. They were also concerned that homosexuality might be hereditary, and if some homosexuals did reproduce, there would be an even larger gay population. For the Nazi leaders, the only way to solve this problem was to get rid of homosexuals. This was accomplished through revisions to Paragraph 175.

In 1935, the following revised text came into effect:

PARAGRAPH 175

175. A male who commits lewd and lascivious acts with another male or permits himself to be so abused for lewd and lascivious acts, shall be punished by imprisonment. In a case of a participant under 21 years of age at the time of the commission of the act, the court may, in especially slight cases, refrain from punishment.

175a. Confinement in a penitentiary not to exceed ten years and, under extenuating circumstances, imprisonment for not less than three months shall be imposed:

1. Upon a male who, with force or *with threat* of imminent danger to life and limb, compels another male to commit lewd and lascivious acts with him or compels the other party to submit to abuse for lewd and lascivious acts;
2. Upon a male who, by abuse of a relationship of dependence upon him, in consequence of service, employment, or subordination, induces another male to commit lewd and lascivious acts with him or to submit to being abused for such, acts;
3. Upon a male who being over 21 years of age induces another male under 21 years of age to commit lewd and lascivious acts with him or to submit to being abused for such acts;
4. Upon a male who professionally engages in lewd and lascivious acts with other men, or submits to such abuse by other men, or offers himself for lewd and lascivious acts with other men.

175b. Lewd and lascivious acts contrary to nature between human beings and animals shall be punished by imprisonment; loss of civil rights may also be imposed. (1)

On June 28, 1935, almost one year to the day after the Night of the Long Knives, revisions to Paragraph 175 were revealed. The Ministry of Justice provided a legal basis for extending the persecution of homosexuals. Criminally indecent activities between men could include nothing more substantial than a touch. The courts later decided that even one's intent, or a homosexual thought, was illegal.

The laws were made retroactive, so that even if an act had occurred years before, the man could still be prosecuted. Homosexuals were targeted for eradication. The Law Against Insidious Slander, which had been passed six months earlier, encouraged relatives and neighbors to spy on one another – making life even more difficult for men who wanted to hide their past activities. Gossip and innuendo became evidence.

Soon it was clear that no one arrested on charges, real or fake, could count on getting a fair trial. Once arrested it was common to torture men to reveal the names of other men who were also homosexual. These "deviants" were to be locked up or sent to concentration camps.

▼

The hunt for homosexuals was orchestrated by Heinrich Himmler, one of the men who had removed Ernst Röhm from his position of strength with Adolf Hitler. With Röhm gone, Himmler's authority increased, and he eventually became the ruthless mass murderer responsible for the deaths of millions. For German homosexuals, Himmler was the greatest enemy.

Appearances can be deceiving, and this was never more apparent than with Heinrich Himmler. Although Himmler was one of the most powerful men in Germany, you wouldn't have known it to look at him. He was often described as looking like a school teacher or an accountant. Himmler was respected as an efficient administrator who kept meticulous records. He started in 1929 as the head of Hitler's bodyguard, the SS, and later oversaw all police and security forces including the Gestapo (Secret State Police). Himmler became the overseer of the concentration

Heinrich Himmler, wearing a Nazi party lapel pin in the 1920s and his 1930s Nazi uniform, had a meek and mild appearance that belied his true nature.

and extermination camps, as well as of the *Einsatzgruppen*, the mobile killing squads that murdered millions of people.

Himmler had originally trained as a farmer and in the early 1920s had tried his hand at poultry farming. While his efforts in farming were unsuccessful, his understanding of animal breeding proved useful in promoting the superiority of the Aryan race. To keep Germany strong, the country had to produce more children. The children, of course, were to be perfect – Aryan and without any physical or mental handicaps. Handicapped children would be eradicated. Homosexuality would also lead to the decline of the German people. Sex between two people was not a private affair but a matter of great national concern.

Himmler stated, "Roughly seven to eight percent of men in Germany are homosexual. If that is how things remain, our nation will fall to pieces because of that plague. Those who practice homosexuality deprive Germany of the children they owe her." (2)

In ancient Germany, homosexuals had been drowned in bogs. Himmler did not think that this should be considered punishment: for him, the murder of homosexual men was the extermination of "abnormal" existence.

Once Ernst Röhm and the SA had been eliminated, Himmler actively consolidated his power and pursued his reign of terror over homosexuals in Germany. In 1934, he was proud to report that "we are not afraid to fight against this plague within our own ranks.... In our judgment of homosexuality – a symptom of racial degeneracy destructive to our race –

we have returned to the guiding Nordic principle that degenerates should be exterminated. Germany stands or falls with the purity of its race."[(3)]

▼

During one six-week period in 1934, the Berlin police under Heinrich Himmler arrested more homosexuals than the German police had in the fifteen years before the Nazis came to power. And that was just the beginning.

The five years from 1935 to 1939 saw the largest number of arrests of homosexuals in Germany. Although Paragraph 175 may not have been strictly enforced prior to the Nazi regime, the police knew the names of many men who were suspected of being homosexual. Since 1900, the police had compiled so-called pink lists containing the names of men throughout the country. These lists were used by the Nazi regime to round up suspected homosexuals. Once arrested, the men would receive a brief trial; many were repeatedly tortured to provide the names of other homosexuals. Police raided homosexual meeting places and seized the address books of arrested men, hoping to find additional suspects. Networks of informers also provided names for the lists.

Police were told how to identify homosexuals; they would likely have feminine appearances and mincing movements; they were supposed to like makeup and perfume; and some enjoyed wearing women's clothing. But these instructions were based on commonly held prejudices. Ernst Röhm, for instance, was a rough and rugged man who never would have been identified as homosexual under these guidelines. As for women, Himmler felt that they should dress in a feminine fashion. If they wore mannish garments, this too could lead to homosexuality within the male population. Women who had previously been comfortable with short hair and masculine suits reconsidered their style of dress.

On October 26, 1936, Himmler formed the Reich Central Office to Combat Homosexuality and Abortion. Tying homosexuality to abortion clearly focused attention on the need to reduce the number of men not interested in making babies and made it illegal for women to not want to have children.

The number of men convicted of charges of homosexuality leapt dramatically after 1935. This chart illustrates the sharp increase in the number of convictions during the first ten years of the Nazi regime:

1933	853
1934	948
1935	2,106
1936	5,320
1937	8,271
1938	8,562
1939	7,614
1940	3,773
1941	3,735
1942	3,963

The years with the highest number of convictions were 1937, 1938, and 1939. The reduction in 1940 reflects a variety of factors: fewer men were living in the cities due to the war effort and greater attention was being paid to the persecution of Jews.

Paragraph 175 had been revised to be so loosely defined that any man could be arrested, charged, and convicted. The Nazis used the law to eliminate anyone that they wanted to be rid of. Even heterosexual men were in danger of arrest if they had made enemies with the Nazis. Catholic clergy were targeted for arrest, not because of suspected rampant homosexuality, but because it was the easiest way to arrest them. Even the Army Chief of Staff, General Werner Von Fritsch was arrested on trumped-up charges under Paragraph 175. The charges against him were finally dropped, but he wisely retired from the Army.

The homosexual population proved to be more difficult to find and arrest than people of a religious group like the Jews or the Jehovah's Witnesses. There was usually no documented proof of homosexuality. There were no birth records to prove someone was a homosexual. A man could pretend not to be homosexual, but his past activities could always be researched. Pierre Seel was a young man arrested when the Nazis discovered his name on a pink list in France.

Pierre was an elegant young Frenchman who liked to dress in the flamboyant "Zazou" style popular at the time. Devotees of the fashion were scattered around the country, but the real cadré of Zazou followers was in Paris. The men wore their hair long, slicked down with Vaseline, and pulled back at the neck. They wore large jackets with multiple pockets and many belts. The jackets were much larger than the typical jackets

This 1930s cartoon illustrates the Zazou style that was adopted by Pierre Seel.

of the day and were viewed as a sign of resistance by some and a sign of decadence by others. The young Zazous were known for their interest in jazz and swing music. Pierre considered his style sophisticated.

The young Pierre Seel had grown up in a devout Catholic family in Mulhouse in France's Alsace region, where his family ran a popular and profitable pâtisserie. During his early teen years, Pierre struggled with his Catholic faith while discovering his attraction to men. By the time he turned seventeen, he was flaunting his individuality through his Zazou style and was actively exploring his homosexuality. On his way home from school, he often stopped at Steinbach Square, a spot known as a homosexual cruising area. There was a café on the square with a second floor that was used for sexual encounters. On one occasion, while he was with a stranger, Pierre realized that his watch had been stolen by his anonymous partner. Pierre called out, but the thief managed to escape. The watch had been a gift from an aunt in Paris for Pierre's communion. He was anxious to get it back, so he reported the theft to the police. That report changed his life forever.

The police officer demanded all the details. When Pierre revealed that the theft occurred in Steinbach Square, the officer berated him for frequenting the square and asked how Pierre thought his father would feel if he knew that his son had been a visitor there. Pierre didn't want to stain the family reputation; he had gone to the police believing he was a victim, but at the police station he had become a humiliated homosexual. The officer assured Pierre that nothing would come of his compromising affair, but warned him to stay away from the square. Pierre left the station feeling ashamed. He didn't realize that his name had been added to a list of the city's homosexuals – a pink list that would later be delivered to the Nazis.

Pierre grew tired of casual encounters and soon found himself spending more and more time with a kind and good young man named Jo. As much as the teens tried, they could not isolate themselves from the rest of the world; in June 1940, life in France drastically changed when the Germans invaded. The Nazis swarmed through Mulhouse.

On May 2, 1941, Pierre's mother told him that the Gestapo had come by the pâtisserie, and that he was to report to the Gestapo headquarters first thing in the morning. When he arrived, he was shoved into a room with other young men who frequented Steinbach Square. The Nazis had used the pink list that the police had compiled to begin the hunt for homosexuals in Mulhouse. One by one the young men were interrogated. The Gestapo called Pierre a filthy faggot and demanded that he provide information about other homosexual men in the city.

It was not a simple interrogation: the men were tortured repeatedly. Some had their fingernails pulled out; Pierre was raped. At dusk they were sent to the prison in Mulhouse. Pierre described the scene in prison: "There were so many [prisoners] that they sat on the ground, leaning against the wall. I had time to see that many of them had likewise been severely tortured; their faces were swollen, their bodies splattered with blood." (4) That first night in prison Pierre couldn't fall asleep; he simply collapsed in exhaustion. For ten days he was held in the city jail, and though his father and brother came to the prison, they were told that he was a queer and there was nothing they could do to help him.

Then, Pierre was transferred with a dozen other prisoners by police van to a concentration camp. From the van the prisoners could see the double rows of high fences with observation towers. Immediately, the prisoners were taunted and beaten, leaving them scared to death. Pierre's Zazou hairstyle singled him out immediately for special treatment. His long hair was shaved off leaving the pattern of a swastika. Pierre's prison uniform had a small blue bar used to identify people who were unwilling to mix socially, or who were Catholics or homosexuals. He was put in barracks that were built to house forty-five men but were now holding more than three times that many. The men slept on sacks of straw over wooden pallets. The upper bunks and those close to the stove were the preferred positions since the evenings were cold even in the spring, due to the high altitude of the camp.

Pierre soon learned the horrors of life in the camp. At 6 a.m. he and his fellow prisoners were awakened, and after a breakfast of moldy bread and indefinable tea, they were sent to the quarries to smash rocks for the next twelve hours. Of his time in the camp Pierre wrote, "I made sure not to talk to anyone, locking myself up in a desperate solitude untouched by any sexual desire. In that place there was no room for even the thought of desire. A ghost has no fantasies, no sexuality." (5) He thought he saw a few men from Mulhouse, but he found it hard to recognize them, "for our clothes, our shaved heads, and our starved

Prisoners at forced labor in the Mauthausen concentration camp. Beginning in 1943, homosexuals were among those in concentration camps who were killed in an SS-sponsored "extermination through work" program.

bodies had erased each man's age and identity. He had become a staggering shadow of himself." (6)

Life in the camp was made more terrifying by the loudspeakers that called men to report for any number of reasons. Pierre was often summoned to participate in medical experiments. In a white room, he and others were lined up against a wall and had needles injected into their nipples – an experiment that killed at least one inmate when the needle struck his heart.

But of all the terrors and horrors in the camp, none could compare to the day on which Pierre saw Jo, his love from only a few months past. He had never seen him before in the camp, but now, at the roll-call site, he knew his friend was about to die. The SS officers stripped him naked and shoved a tin pail over his head. They then let their well-trained German Shepherd dogs loose. All the prisoners were forced to watch as the dogs attacked and killed Jo.

Pierre endured the hellish rhythm of camp life until November 1941. When he heard the camp authorities call "Seel, Peter" over the dreaded loudspeakers, he feared he was going to be punished because he had stolen some carrots when he was assigned to clean the rabbit hutches a few days before. Instead, he was shocked to learn that he was to be released due to his good behavior. However, he had to sign a document agreeing never to speak about what he had experienced in the camp.

Still only eighteen, Pierre Seel returned to his family with a shaved head and a gaunt body. He had endured a great deal, but his family never spoke of his ordeals, or of his homosexuality. Months later, in March 1942, Pierre received his German draft notice and was sent to Vienna for military training. That began his crisscrossing of Europe as a soldier fighting against the enemies of Germany, the very people he wanted to support.

The Nazis were able to build on the prejudices of previous generations to gain support for their hatred of homosexuals. Everyone was encouraged to help rid the population of the filthy queers in much the same way as people were encouraged to help identify and persecute the Jews. For a homosexual man, there was no one to trust. Half the arrests were the result of reports from private individuals. Hotel owners phoned the police, and passersby might report what they had seen on the street. Homosexuals were not safe in their own homes. One woman, frustrated by a relationship that seemed to be going nowhere, denounced her boyfriend and a friend of his as lovers to the police.

Anonymous letters arrived at the Gestapo identifying men as homosexuals. "We have lived in the same house for twelve years, but in all that time he has never been out with a girl. Obviously I cannot say anything for certain, but it strikes me as very suspicious. What are all these young men doing there? But I must ask you not to disclose my name." (7)

Another report stated that "office employee Max P. says that on 31 July 1940 he saw Doctor L. letting a young male person into his home. Shortly after that, he closed the curtains of his bedroom." (8)

Such reports led to arrests, convictions, and often death.

Homosexual men didn't know whom to trust when trying to hide their sexuality. As previously mentioned, some married lesbians, others married sympathetic female friends, and almost all tried to hide their sexuality as carefully as they could. Men joined the army believing that there was less attention paid to the hunt for homosexuals in the armed forces. However, if a man in the armed forces was found to be sexually involved with another man, he could be immediately executed.

Himmler estimated that there were two million homosexual men in Germany. This number was considered a gross exaggeration, but even if there were only one quarter of this number – 500,000 – the fact that there were only 100,000 to 150,000 arrests indicates that many homosexuals were able to hide their preference for the same sex.

▼

In 1938 the Gestapo issued a directive stating that a man convicted of gross indecency could be transferred directly to a concentration camp instead of going to prison. In 1940 Himmler added an amendment to this directive, stating that men who had seduced more than two men *must* be transferred to a concentration camp after serving their prison sentences.

After the war began in 1939, Himmler's attention was more focused on the extermination of the Jews than on the persecution of homosexuals. Homosexuals were still targeted, but there were millions of others who were falling to the wrath of the Nazis. Still, by 1941, Himmler was acting with more severity against homosexuals. It was announced that any SS or police officer engaging in indecent behavior with another man would be condemned to death. Himmler had not been given any authority over the men in the army and navy, but this changed in 1943 when he proclaimed that the SS had complete jurisdiction over soldiers and sailors convicted of same-sex indecent behavior. Thus, even more homosexuals could be executed.

CHAPTER 5

Death through Work – Imprisonment in the Concentration Camps

Over the gates of many concentration camps were the words *Arbeit Macht Frei,* which translates as Work Makes You Free. But gay men arriving at the camps soon learned that the work they would be given would most likely kill them. Millions of Jews and hundreds of thousands of Roma were sent to the gas chambers after walking through these gates, but because the men arrested under Paragraph 175 were German Christians, they were spared that fate, only to die through work.

The brutal treatment that a prisoner experienced upon arrest was just a taste of the horror that awaited him in a concentration camp (the name comes from the "concentration" of those imprisoned there). The camps were used as prisons and labor centers for the enemies of the state. As the number of people arrested by the Nazis increased, the number

The gates at Sachsenhausen concentration camp.

of camps grew. The first was Dachau, northwest of Munich, and during the next few years more were added: Oranienburg, north of Berlin; Esterwegen, near Hamburg; Buchenwald, near Weimar; Flossenbürg, close to the border with Czechoslovakia; Mauthausen, in upper Austria; and Ravensbrück (for women) and Sachsenhausen, both close to Berlin. The locations were crucial as the camps provided forced labor for mines, quarries, and factories; by 1942 the prisoners were being used to produce weapons for the German war effort.

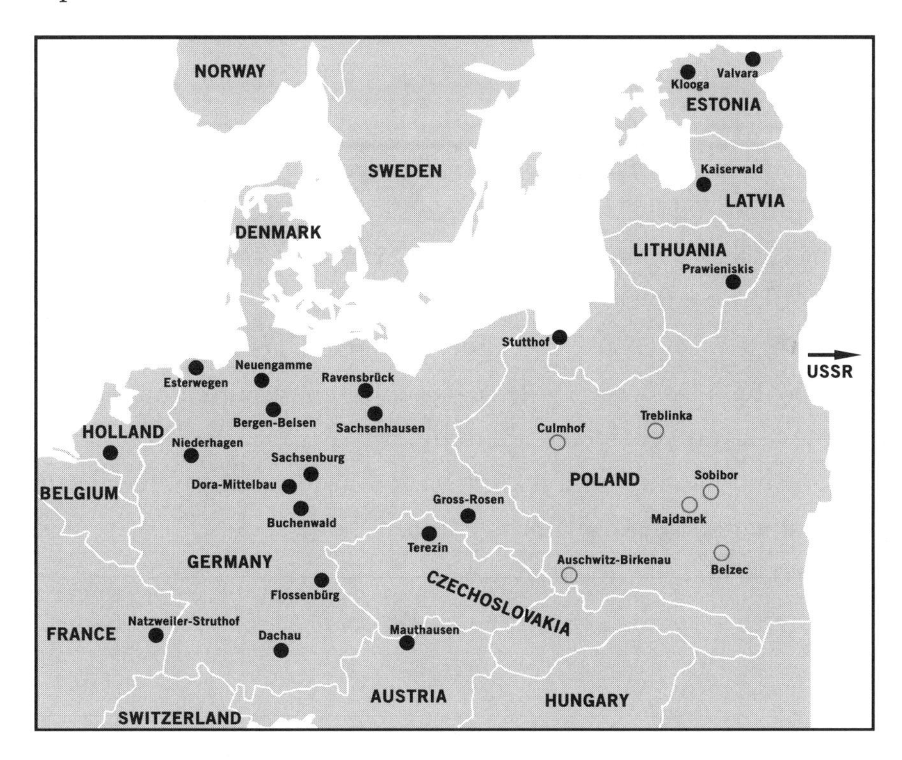

Nazi concentration camps (solid black dots) were scattered around Europe. The major death camps were located in Nazi-occupied Poland.

Other camps were used for the efficient murder of Jews. Six sites were selected in Poland because they were close to railroad lines and were located in remote rural areas. The camps at Chełmno, Belzec, Sobibor, Treblinka, Majdanek, and Auschwitz were known as extermination or death camps. There, most arrivals were sent directly to the gas chambers.

The conditions for all prisoners were barbaric and grew worse with each passing year. The work was backbreaking, the barracks were bleak, and food rations could barely keep a person alive. Every day prisoners were forced to witness executions of other prisoners by shooting or hanging. Guards controlled the prisoners with a casual brutality. Survival was difficult for any prisoner.

On arrival at a camp, each prisoner became a number and a colored symbol. Yellow was for Jews, red for political figures, green for criminals, black for anti-socials, purple for Jehovah's Witnesses, blue for non-German forced laborers, brown for Roma. And, of course, the pink triangle for men arrested under Paragraph 175.

Why pink was used for homosexuals remains unknown. It could be that pink was considered a feminine color, much as it is today, and would be humiliating for a man to wear. But that is simply conjecture. No documentation is available to confirm the reason that pink triangles were used to identify homosexuals.

RIGHT: This chart shows the various prisoner markings used in the concentration camps.

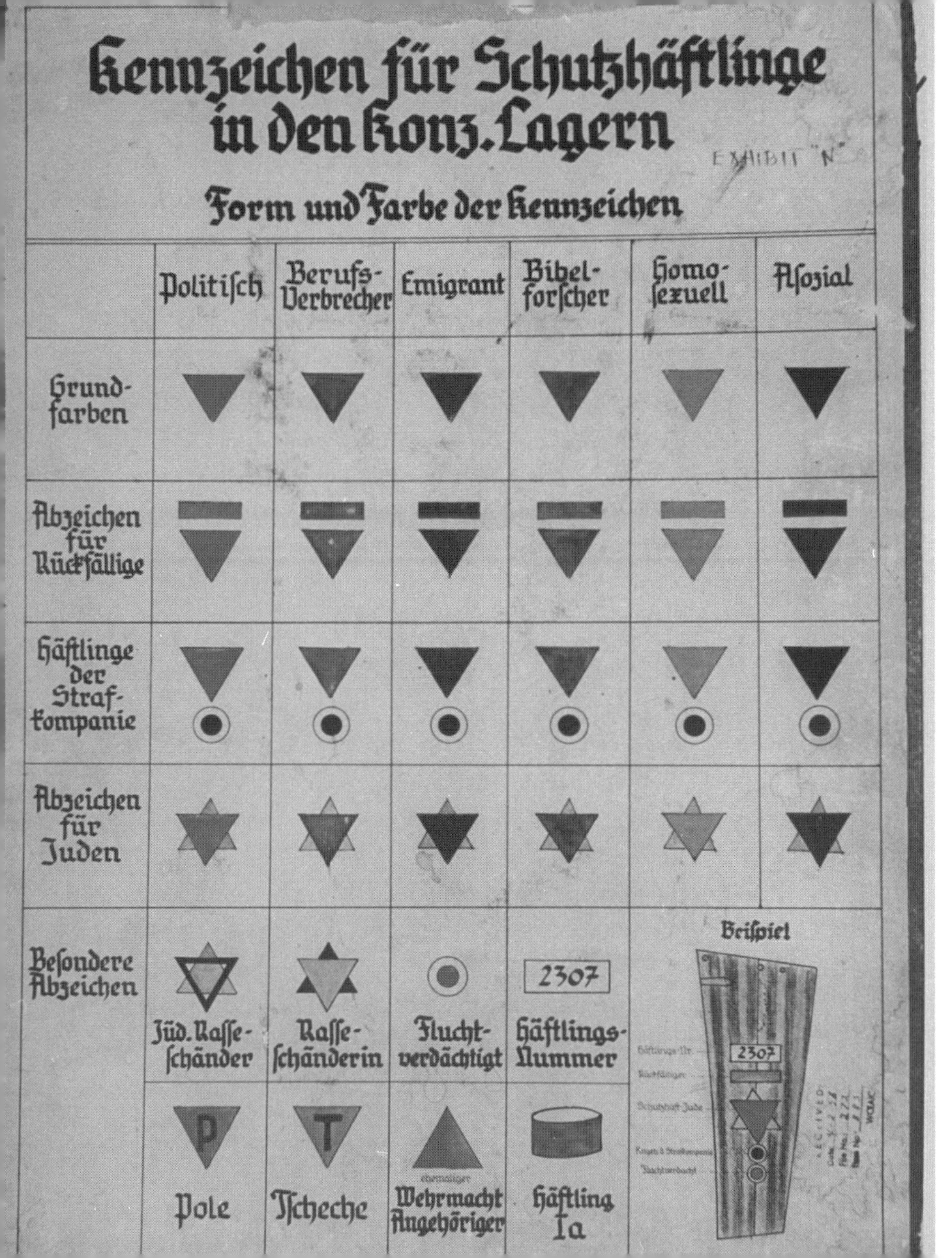

Kennzeichen für Schutzhäftlinge in den Konz. Lagern

EXHIBIT "N"

Form und Farbe der Kennzeichen

	Politisch	Berufs-Verbrecher	Emigrant	Bibelforscher	Homosexuell	Asozial
Grundfarben						
Abzeichen für Rückfällige						
Häftlinge der Strafkompanie						
Abzeichen für Juden						

Besondere Abzeichen				
	Jüd. Rasseschänder	Rasseschänderin	Fluchtverdächtigt	2307 Häftlings-Nummer
	P Pole	T Tscheche	ehemaliger Wehrmacht Angehöriger	Häftling Ia

Beispiel

2307

Schutzhaft Jude

▼

Lesbians who were arrested and sent to concentration camps did not wear the pink triangle. They wore the black triangle as anti-social prisoners. Researcher Claudia Schoppmann studied the fate of lesbians and reported the following:

> The number of women who were subjected to the horrors of the concentration camps because they were lesbians cannot be documented. What is definitive is that there was no systematic persecution of lesbians that was comparable to the persecution of gay men. Most lesbians were spared a fate in the camps if they were willing to conform. Lesbians were not victims of the Nazi regime per se. (1)

Homosexuals were not only the targets of abuse and violence from the guards, but they also suffered abuse at the hands of other frustrated and angry prisoners. One survivor described the pecking order in the Schirmeck-Vorbruck camp. "There was a hierarchy from the strongest to the weakest. There was no doubt that the weakest in the camps were the homosexuals. All the way to the bottom." (2)

When the guards discovered that a prisoner was homosexual, he was often targeted for harsh treatment. "Because of my pink triangle I was separated from other inmates," reported one man who was a prisoner at Camp Natzweiler close to Strasbourg, France. "An SS sergeant together with a kapo mistreated me in the most brutal manner...three times their fists hit my face, especially my nose, so that I fell on the floor three times; when I managed to get up again, they continued battering and beating me.... I then staggered back to my barracks covered with blood." [3]

In many camps homosexuals were housed apart because the Nazis believed that homosexuality was a disease that could spread to the other prisoners. At night in the barracks the lights were left on so that the guards could monitor behavior. The men were forced to sleep with their hands on top of their blankets to prove that they were not masturbating. If a man was caught asleep with his hands under the covers, he could be sent outside naked, have a bucket of water poured over him, and made to stand for hours – even in the dead of winter. A particularly painful punishment was being suspended by the wrists on posts, with the arms tied behind the back.

A prisoner at the Sachsenhausen concentration camp described the sound the prisoners made when they were suspended from the poles as the "Singing Forest – the howling and the screaming were inhuman... inexplicable. Beyond comprehension." [4]

The odds against survival were huge, but the odds improved if one could find a kapo. There were cases when a kapo might help a young gay prisoner in exchange for sexual favors, but these relationships were always at the whim of the kapo. And the kapo could always find a new "dolly boy," as they were called, from the recent arrivals, and dispose

With their arms tied behind their backs, prisoners were supended by the wrists from these poles, which still stand at Sachsenhausen concentration camp.

Artist Richard Grune was prosecuted under Paragraph 175, and from 1937 was incarcerated in concentration camps. In 1947 he produced a series of etchings detailing what he had witnessed in the camps. This one is titled "Solidarity."

of the previous one easily. Being a "dolly boy" was not an option for older or less attractive men.

Many gay men faced another horror in the medical chambers of the camps. When Richard Plant studied the fate of gay men in the camps, he concluded that Nazi doctors performed experiments on prisoners, and homosexuals were used in disproportionately large numbers for these so-called scientific procedures. (5)

Medical labs, now clean and on view for concentration camp visitors, were the scenes of horrific "scientific" experiments performed on prisoners.

The experiments were performed for a variety of reasons, including finding the cause of homosexuality. The experiments often caused sickness, mutilation, or death. Castration was considered an option to cure homosexuality. Some men were told they would be released from prison if they agreed to be castrated.

Others were not given the option and were castrated without their consent. Toward the end of the war, when Germany was running out of soldiers, pink triangle prisoners were granted a slim chance of survival – if they agreed to castration, they would be allowed out of camp to join the German army at the front. The prisoners knew they were being used as cannon fodder. Serving at the front meant almost certain death.

There are no known statistics for the number of homosexuals who died in the camps, but their death rate has been estimated to be as high as sixty percent – among the highest of non-Jewish prisoners.

▼

A fragile strip of cloth, two inches long and less than an inch wide, with its number and pink triangle sits in the United States Holocaust Museum in Washington, D.C. It is the only pink triangle known to have been worn by a prisoner who can be identified. That prisoner was Josef Kohout, the first survivor to tell the world of the horrors endured by homosexuals in the concentration camps.

Josef Kohout was born into a wealthy Catholic family in Vienna, Austria, in 1917. The family home may have been religious, but it was a tolerant one that respected others, regardless of religion, race, or language. Josef's father held a high-ranking position in the civil service, and the family had great expectations for their son's future. As a teen, Josef was attracted to other boys. He tried going out with girls, but he knew deep down that he preferred to be with boys.

Josef kept his feelings to himself, although by the time he was nineteen, he was sure that he was homosexual. Because he had difficulty living with this secret, he told his mother, hoping for her support. Her response did not disappoint him. "My dear child," she told him, "it's your life, and you must live it. No one can slip out of one skin and into another; you have to make the best of what you are...you are my son and can always come to me with your problems." [6]

Josef was twenty-two when he went to university to further his

A tiny, fragile strip of cloth with its number and pink triangle sits in the United States Holocaust Museum in Washington, D.C. It is the only pink triangle known to have been worn by a prisoner who can be identified. That prisoner was Josef Kohout.

studies in the hope of becoming an academic. He quickly found a group of friends with similar interests, and within that group he fell in love with the son of a high Nazi official. Fred was two years older than Josef and was studying medicine at Vienna's world famous medical school. Josef found much to admire in Fred, with his forceful personality, masculine appearance, and athletic body. And Fred was smitten with Josef's Viennese charm and his athleticism. The two young men fell into a comfortable relationship and planned their future together – a future that was never to happen.

On a Friday in March of 1939 at about 1 p.m., the Gestapo came to the Kohout home and summoned Josef to Gestapo headquarters at the Hotel Metropol for a meeting at 2 p.m., only an hour later. Josef was concerned, but didn't think it was anything very serious. He figured that if it had been serious, he would have been taken right away. Still, he was apprehensive, as was his mother. Her last words were, "Be careful child, be careful." (7) Josef left home never realizing that he would not see his mother or anyone else in his family for another six years.

At Gestapo headquarters, Josef was ushered in to see an SS doctor. He stood waiting while the doctor continued to write at his desk. When the doctor finally looked up, he stared at Josef with cold, appraising eyes and said, "You are a queer, a homosexual. Do you admit it?" Josef was shocked and denied the accusation.

"Don't you lie, you dirty queer!" the doctor warned. "I have proof." (8)

He showed Josef a photo of Josef and Fred with their arms around each other's shoulders in a friendly fashion. On the back of the photo was an inscription: "To my friend Fred, in eternal love and deepest affection!" Josef had given the photo to Fred the previous Christmas and now the photo was being used to condemn him as a homosexual.

The doctor passed Josef a document to sign confirming his homosexuality. There was nothing Josef could do but sign – the photo from 1938 was all the proof the Nazis needed. Josef was sent immediately to the police prison. When he asked if he could call his family from prison, he was told they would learn soon enough that he was not coming home.

His trial was held two weeks later, and he was sentenced to six months labor by the Austrian court for his homosexual behavior. Fred was also accused, but the charges were later dropped on the grounds of "mental confusion." It was assumed that Fred was spared because his father was a high-ranking Nazi and had somehow managed to get his son out of trouble.

Josef was transferred to the Vienna district prison to serve his sentence; for six months he did domestic work, washing, cleaning, and delivering meals to prisoners. At the end of his term, however, instead of being released he was informed that he would be sent to a concentration camp – a destination of which he had only heard rumors. He hoped that the stories of people being tortured to death were exaggerations.

In January of 1940, Josef was transported by train to the camp at Sachsenhausen, on the outskirts of Berlin. Prisoners were packed into cattle cars with heavily barred windows. The worst criminals were segregated in specially designed cars, each containing five or six barred cells. Josef was ordered into one of those cells with two other men – thieves

Pink triangle prisoners marched to the parade ground under the watchful eyes of Nazi guards.

who were scheduled to be executed for murder. When the two killers discovered that Josef was a "175er," a "filthy queer," they treated him with contempt and taunted him mercilessly. The trip lasted thirteen days, and Josef feared for his life each day. The men beat him regularly and, though they were so-called "normal" men, forced him to provide sex.

At the camp, the men in the transport were unloaded on the parade ground. They formed up in rows of five, for a roll call. One by one, each man was ordered to step forward and give his name and offence. When Josef announced he was arrested under Paragraph 175, the SS officer in charge gave him a violent blow to the face and threw him on the ground.

"You filthy queer, get over there!" he shouted. (9)

Other prisoners warned Josef to get up quickly or he would be kicked to death. All the "175ers" were herded to their block, stripped naked, and forced to stand barefoot in the snow. The SS officer, in his warm winter coat complete with fur collar, repeatedly struck the naked men with his horse whip, telling them that they would stay there until they cooled off. When they were finally allowed to go into the showers, they discovered that the water was ice cold. Josef was issued prison clothing. His trousers were too short, his jacket too small, but luckily his coat actually fit. His shoes were too large and reeked of sweat, but at least they were leather instead of the wooden shoes that many of the other prisoners received.

Homosexuals were housed in one barrack where they were under almost constant surveillance. The block contained about 250 men in each wing – unskilled workers, shop assistants, skilled tradesmen, musicians, artists, professors, aristocratic landowners, and even clergy. The lights stayed on all night, and here, too, the men had to keep their hands on top of the blankets.

Most of the other prisoners at Sachsenhausen were political prisoners or enemies of the state. Those with pink triangles were not allowed to speak to the other prisoners; if they were caught within 4.5 meters (5 yards) of the other barracks, the punishment was a brutal whipping of fifteen to twenty strokes.

The days in the camp were grueling, beginning at 6 a.m. in the winter, or 5 a.m. in the summer. The length of a day's work followed the amount of available sunlight. The most feared job was at the nearby brickworks, known as the death pit. It was here that Josef was sent. The working conditions were lethal, fatalities a routine daily occurrence.

No one was spared the camp's brutal treatment. At the end of February, after he had been at Sachsenhausen for only a few weeks, Josef witnessed the arrival of a sixty-year-old Catholic priest. This tall, distinguished man came from an aristocratic German family. The arrival process, with its long, naked wait in the snow, was particularly difficult for him. When he was finally allowed to go to the barracks, his scalp bleeding from the rough shaving of his hair, he started to pray. The priest's praying was reported to the SS who forced the other prisoners to watch as the priest was tied to a bench and beaten unconscious.

At morning roll call the next day – a dull, overcast day – when everyone was to assemble for roll call, the priest had to be carried to the parade ground. When the SS block sergeant raised his hand to beat the priest anew, a single ray of sunshine shone down on the priest's battered face.

All the men on the parade ground, including the sergeant, looked to the sky. The ray of sunshine shone only on the priest. The sergeant let his hand fall to his side. By evening the priest lay dead. Deeply religious, Josef remembered the death of the priest and that single ray of sunshine the rest of his life.

Many pink triangle prisoners died from the harsh working conditions in the Sachenhausen brickworks.

Josef's next job was just as horrendous as working at the brickworks. He was chosen to be part of a group that was to build a new firing range for the SS. Each day the men had to build the range while the SS practiced with their rifles. The SS preferred to practice with live targets. More than fifteen men were shot during the building of the range. Luckily, Josef was transferred out of the firing-range detail when he reluctantly agreed to provide sexual favors to one of the camp kapos. Josef had decided that his will to survive was far stronger than his commitment to decency;

while it may have been degrading to have sex with the kapo, he believed it would help keep him alive.

In May 1940, Josef, only twenty-three, was transferred to the Flossenbürg concentration camp. He quickly learned that one camp was as bad as another, but he was determined to survive. He soon attracted the attention of a prison block senior – a kapo of importance and a ruthless safecracker. The man got young Josef an easy job as a clerk, and provided him with much-needed extra rations. The safecracker saved Josef's life several times, but when he was transferred to another block, their relationship ended. Josef had no difficulty finding another kapo.

By 1942, Kohout himself was made a kapo – one of the few pink triangle kapos in the camps. He was put in charge of a group of men in the munitions factory. Since all able-bodied men were fighting for Germany, prisoners from the concentration camps now worked in the factories. The pink triangles were still considered degenerate, but manpower was desperately needed to keep the munitions factories operating. Josef created a strong work force in the camp, ensuring not only his survival, but also the survival of the men in his crew. He developed a system of instructions using numbers instead of German, making it possible for those who didn't understand German to work and keep the factory operating.

In the summer of 1943, a prison brothel was established in Flossenbürg. This was part of Himmler's bizarre idea of how to "cure" homosexuality. All pink triangle prisoners were compelled to make visits to the brothel to learn the joys of sex with women. The brothel was staffed with Jewish and Roma women from the Ravensbrück camp. They had been promised that after six months of service, they would be released. In reality, after their six months, they were shipped off to the Auschwitz gas chambers. Josef went to the brothel on occasion, but his brief visits did nothing to alter his sexual orientation.

Not surprisingly, the project was a dismal failure.

As the war effort continued to go badly for Germany through 1943, the need for soldiers grew, and Josef and others were offered the opportunity to have themselves castrated so that they could fight on the Russian front. When the camp commandant asked Josef if he had agreed to be castrated, Josef answered that he wanted to go home in the same state he came in. The camp commandant replied, "You and the whole pack of you queers, you're never going to go home again." (10)

But Josef Kohout did go home. At the war's end he was still alive: he had survived six years in the concentration camps. He had never even said good-bye to his family in 1939. In the summer of 1945, a thin and drawn Josef Kohout made his way back to Vienna to see his mother. He had already discovered that his father had repeatedly tried to secure his release, or at least to visit to him, but had never been successful. Josef's father had eventually committed suicide.

CHAPTER 6

Nazis in Occupied Territories

Hitler's preoccupation was increasingly focused on building a new master race of Germans. Policies toward homosexuals living in occupied countries varied. If the area was populated by people deemed to be of the superior Nordic race, such as the Alsatians in France, the Austrians, and the Dutch in the Netherlands, then Paragraph 175 was introduced into the laws of the occupied territory, and homosexuals were actively pursued. The population was to be cleansed of such men, since they would weaken the male Aryan population.

However, in countries like Poland and in parts of the Soviet Union, where the population was deemed inferior, the Nazis did not bother to target homosexuals but left them alone, believing that they would help destroy the society from within. That said, when homosexuals were found in these countries, they could still be brutalized or imprisoned. And there was always the possibility of torture, or even death.

The story of Polish Stefan Kosinski reveals the brutality of the Nazis in occupied territories.

▼

Stefan Kosinski was only fourteen when the Nazis invaded Poland in 1939. Almost immediately, his life was upended. He didn't know where his father was, but had heard that he had been sent to a labor camp in Germany. Stefan, along with his four siblings and his mother, had been forced from their simple apartment into one room in a rundown old building. He would never get to wear his new school uniform because the Nazis had closed the schools. But Stefan believed that he had much to be thankful for.

He had been lucky enough to get a job as a delivery boy for a German baker. Not only did a job with a German employer reduce the risk of deportation to the forced-labor camps, but also the leftover bread and rolls he received helped him feed the family. Stefan had a beautiful singing voice and was thrilled when he landed a part-time position with a local opera company. Only Germans were allowed to have singing roles, so Stefan served as a member of the chorus. Still, it was a chance to be on stage, where he could sense the excitement of the theater and feel valued for his talents. The opera also provided Stefan with a pass that allowed him to be on the streets of Toruń after the eight o'clock curfew for non-Germans.

One night in November 1941, he was walking home after the opera. It was cold and a layer of soft, white snow covered the ground. Stefan sensed that someone was watching him as he walked the dark and empty streets. When he finally saw the man, he became nervous. It was a soldier, and Stefan knew soldiers could make life miserable for him, even though he had a pass. But this soldier didn't seem to want to make things difficult. He smiled at Stefan, and after walking past each other a few times, he greeted Stefan with "good evening" instead of "Heil Hitler" and shook his hand. Stefan noticed that the soldier had held his hand a little longer than was usual, and when the soldier invited him to a café so that they wouldn't have to stand in the street talking, he quickly accepted.

At the café, Stefan, with his limited German, admitted to being Polish. This could have meant immediate arrest, but the soldier was relieved that Stefan had a pass. Still, just being in the café was against the law for Stefan, and being with a Polish youth past curfew was not something that a young soldier should have been doing either.

Over coffee, the soldier said that he was Austrian and that his name was Willi. They stayed until after midnight when the café closed. Stefan believed that this was a one-time chance encounter. But Willi was anxious to see Stefan again, and the two agreed to meet the next night after the opera.

The two met again the next night, and then each night after that, walking through the less-traveled streets of Toruń, telling each other about themselves. November in Poland can mean changeable weather, and the snow had melted during a thaw. The warmer weather made the walks more comfortable, but the ground had become muddy, slippery, and almost treacherous, especially on the less-busy streets they sought out. On a late night walk just outside the city, Stefan stepped into a mud hole and lost his shoe. Willi, in his sturdy army-issue boots, picked Stefan up and carried him to dry ground. They walked a short distance up a path off the road and came upon an abandoned shed.

It was in the shed that Willi first kissed Stefan. The shed became their refuge from the world, a place where they could meet regularly away from prying eyes. Willi told Stefan he wanted to take Stefan to his home in Vienna after the war, where they could live a life together without uniforms.

In April, Willi learned that his unit was being deployed to the Russian front. They both knew what that meant. Very few soldiers ever returned from the Russian front. Willi declared his love and promised he would write to Stefan as soon as he could.

Months passed and no letter arrived. For Stefan, the wait was unbearable. By August he could wait no longer and sent Willi these few lines:

> *Dear Willi,*
> *I haven't had any news at all of you for so long. I'm so worried about it. I miss you so much. I think of you every day. I am always thinking about you. I pray every day that you will come back safe.*

I'm working in the theater as before, but I'm not going out anywhere. Also not to the place we used to meet. I'm just true to you and will remain so for my whole life. Please write to me as quickly as possible so I can be reassured. I can't sleep, I think only of you.

With love and kisses,
Your Stefan [(1)]

Stefan included his return address, believing that the letter would be returned to him if Willi could not be found. It never occurred to him that the letter might be read by anyone other than Willi.

A few weeks later, Stefan was summoned to the local Gestapo headquarters. He was surprised to see that the Gestapo had his letter. They demanded to know if he had written it. He had no choice but to admit that he had. Stefan was stripped, bent over a table, and whipped with belts until blood flowed and he lost consciousness. He was taken to a cell, then dragged out again for further beatings.

The Gestapo shoved photos of men in front of him demanding that he identify other homosexuals. He didn't know any of the men in the photos except for a few he recognized from the theater. Willi had had been his only lover. Stefan was beaten repeatedly, his wounds reopening again and again. He prayed he would die to end the beatings. Finally, after weeks of torture, he was forced to sign a document. Stefan didn't know what he was signing – the document was in German. When his case was finally sent to trial, he saw his mother in the gallery. She listened as he was convicted of being a homosexual who had been a Polish whore to the whole German army.

His sentence? Five years. Stefan Kosinski was still just a teenager.

First he was sent to a forced-labor camp in Stuhm, Germany, and then to a concentration camp in Graudenz, Poland. Like every other camp prisoner, he suffered and witnessed untold horrors. He was still in a concentration camp when his teenage years ended. He had turned twenty in 1945 when he and all the other prisoners were forced on a death march as the Allied forces approached the camp. In the bitter cold of winter, the prisoners walked, knowing that if they fell, they would freeze to death; if they tried to escape, they would be shot. The march ended at a prison in Hanover, Germany. Stefan escaped in 1945, just before liberation.

CHAPTER 7
Jewish Homosexuals

For Jews, the matter of sexuality was of little importance: Jews were targeted for extermination whatever their sexuality. During the first years of the Nazi regime, a gay Jew was more likely to be arrested and punished as a homosexual than as a Jew. But once the Nazis began to persecute the Jews, Jewish homosexuals and lesbians were simply rounded up as Jews. It was easier to hide one's homosexuality than it was to hide the fact that one was Jewish. Still, there were those who were able to go into hiding with the help of friends and support from outside of Germany. Gad Beck, a homosexual Jew, was able to survive through his determination, strong connections, and extreme good luck.

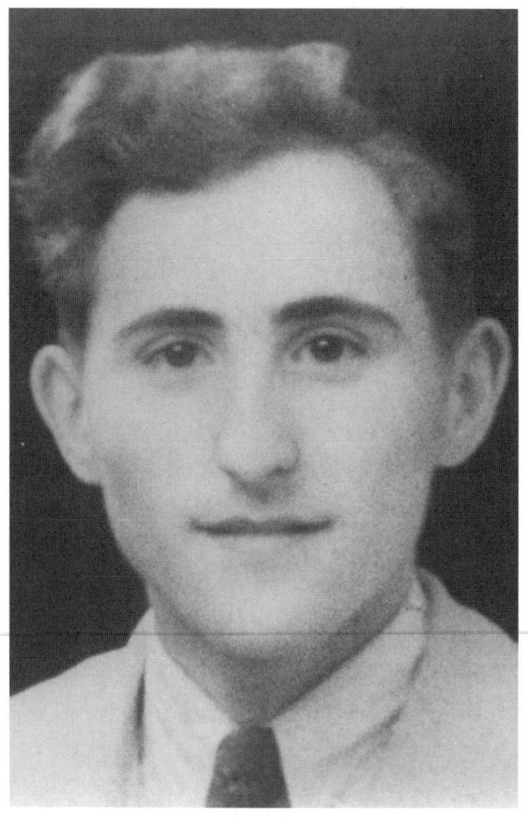

Gad knew from an early age that he was a homosexual.

With an Austrian Jewish father and a Christian German mother who had converted to Judaism, Gad Beck and his twin sister were *mischlings* (only part Aryan) and not as strongly targeted when the Nazis began their assault on the Jews. Gerhard (as he was first named) and his twin sister, Margot (later called Miriam), were born in Berlin in 1923. Gerhard knew from a very early age that he was attracted to boys. He was not sexually shy with males and had many pre-teen and teen crushes on boys and men. His parents were understanding and knew that their son was a homosexual at an early age.

In 1936, when Gerhard turned thirteen, the age at which Jewish boys have their bar mitzvah, the Beck family threw an event for Gad that was to be their last happy family celebration. After that their lives changed for the worse. Gerhard's father lost his job and Gerhard had to go to work because there wasn't enough money for his school tuition. Life was hard for him in the next few years, but it was relatively stable. The Beck family was even able to enjoy the success of an Austrian relative, Walter Beck, who won a bronze medal in the Berlin Olympics.

Twins Gerhard and Margot Beck, seen here on the day of Gerhard's bar mitzvah, were half Aryan and half Jewish. They later changed their names to Gad and Miriam and joined a Zionist training center.

When the Nazis annexed Austria in 1938, life for the Becks changed even more dramatically. They were evicted from their home and forced to find a place in a segregated area for Jews called a *Judenhaus* (Jews' House). The Becks had considered emigration, but by then it was much too late: Jews were not allowed to leave Germany and only those with money and connections could even hope for the chance to go somewhere else. On November 8, 1938, when the riots that became known as *Kristallnacht* destroyed Jewish businesses, residences, and synagogues, it was clear that life for Jews living in Germany would never be the same. By 1939, they were being turned into the slaves of the Nazi regime, and the Jews in Berlin were conscripted to work in the German armaments industry.

Gerhard and his sister had the good fortune of being able to join a *Hachshara,* a Zionist preparation and training center for young people planning to emigrate to Palestine. The Zionists were still running the Hachsharas in 1940, and by 1941, close to 40,000 young Jews had gone to Palestine. Gerhard and Margot were accepted into the program in May of 1940. It was there that they took their Hebrew names, Gad and Miriam. They trained for life in Palestine, but restrictions on emigration made the journey impossible. Though Gad was unable to go to Palestine, he continued to be involved in the Zionist organization.

It was in one of these groups that he fell in love with a young man named Manfred Lewin, whom Gad remembered as being of medium height, athletic, with brown hair and eyes. The two teens were cast in a theatrical reading of the play *Don Carlos*. One weekend, when the group was practicing in the building that was the former Jewish Teacher's Association, they camped out on the roof. They had brought food, sleeping bags, and a guitar. They couldn't go on a camping trip to the country as they had in the past, so this rooftop adventure was the next best thing. That night up on the roof, the two boys kissed. Gad was in love, but Manfred, while also in love, had difficulty accepting their physical relationship. Gad, however, was persuasive and persistent, and they continued their relationship. Around the time of Gad's birthday in June, Manfred admitted to Gad, "With you it's okay." (1) It was to be Gad's best birthday present. They were together through the summer.

In 1941, the Nazis began deporting Jews from Berlin. Gad and Miriam were doing forced labor in the armaments industry. As they were mischlings, they felt a small degree of safety. Still, Gad saw his Jewish friends being deported almost daily. He was aware that some had gone into hiding, but for many Jews it was impossible to leave their parents and grandparents, brothers and sisters. Manfred and his family received their deportation notice in the fall of 1942. Gad knew that he had to act fast. He couldn't imagine a future without Manfred.

Manfred Lewin was Gad's great love.

Gad went to Manfred's employer, a painter named Lothar Hermann. Gad explained that Manfred had been picked up by the Nazis. Hermann had lost many employees in this manner, and he thought well of Manfred. He didn't want to lose a good worker. He told Gad he had an idea – "if you have the nerve." [2] Gad said he would do anything to free Manfred.

Hermann's plan was ingenious, but extremely risky. Hermann had a son who was a member of the Nazi Youth, and he said there was a Nazi uniform in his house that might fit Gad. It didn't. It was actually four sizes too big, but Gad made makeshift alterations tucking up the sleeves and the pants on the inside. He wore the uniform to the assembly hall where the Lewins were being held. The hall was in Gad's old school and was being used to hold Jews prior to their deportation and ultimate death. It was crowded at the entrance where many people were asking about their relatives. Some tried to bribe the guards for their relatives' freedom.

"Heil Hitler!" Gad announced as he arrived and asked to speak to the officer in charge. He quickly made up a story about how Lothar Hermann was renovating apartments and how the Jew, Manfred Lewin, had hidden the keys to several units. Hermann now needed Manfred to show him where the keys were so that the workers could get back to renovating.

The story worked and Manfred was brought out to Gad. The officer instructed Gad to bring Manfred right back.

"What would I want with a Jew?" Gad retorted. (3)

The two boys made their way down the street away from the school. Gad was elated. He had just saved his boyfriend from deportation! Gad gave Manfred twenty marks, telling him to go to his uncle where he would be safe until Gad could come for him.

Manfred shocked Gad when he calmly replied, "I can't go with you. My family needs me. If I abandon them now, I could never be free." (4)

Manfred had made his decision. Without a smile or a tear – without even a good-bye – he turned and went back to be with his family, leaving Gad on the street in his borrowed Nazi uniform. "In those seconds, watching him go, I grew up," wrote Gad years later. (5)

Gad Beck never saw Manfred Lewin again. For the rest of his life, he kept a small notebook given to him by Manfred. In this precious book, Manfred had written poems and notes and made drawings about events in their relationship.

With each passing day, life grew more difficult for Gad, his family, and any Jews living in Berlin. Gad now worked during the day unloading potatoes as they were brought into the city. It was tiring work, but at least he hadn't been deported. What little free time he had was spent assisting in the underground network that helped Jews who had gone into hiding. The network relied on the support of many people. Some helped because it was the right thing to do; others helped for the money they could make; and some assisted because of their anger at the Nazi regime.

In the apartment building where the Beck family lived, there was an unused attic where Gad had taken in other young Jewish men who needed a place to hide, and where he and Manfred met. Gad had always been very careful when bringing anyone home because there was a tenant in the building, a young German named Heinz Bluemel, who constantly wore his Nazi uniform. Heinz was a handsome youth, but had a prominent hump on his back. He kept a careful watch over the goings on in his building. One night when Gad was returning home, the

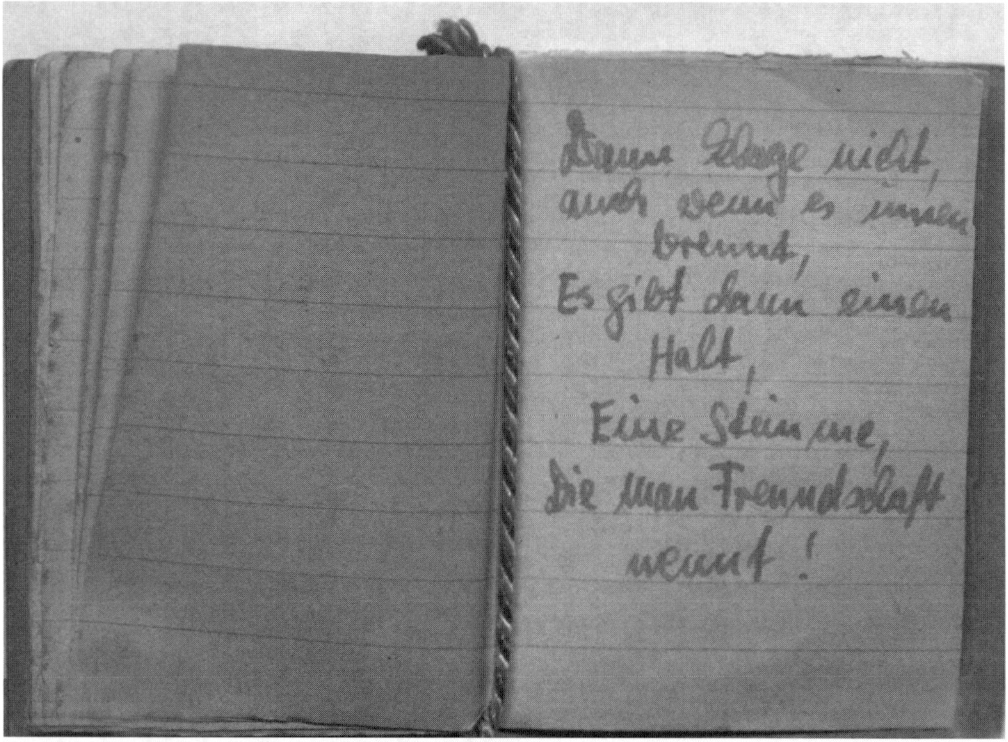

Drum klage nicht,
auch wenn es innen
brennt,
Es gibt dann einen
Halt,
Eine Stimme,
Die man Freundschaft
nennt!

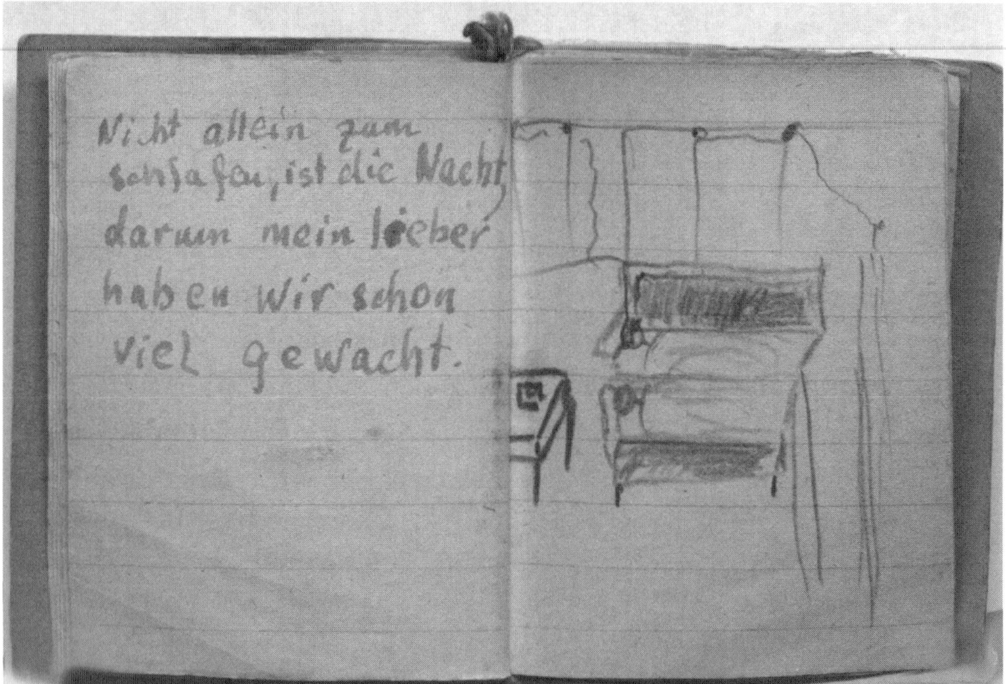

Nicht allein zum
schlafen, ist die Nacht,
darum mein lieber
haben wir schon
viel gewacht.

air-raid sirens began wailing. Heinz, in civilian clothing, hurried Gad to the basement. When the danger ended, Heinz asked Gad to join him on a tour of the building, to make sure there wasn't any damage. It was in the attic that Heinz told Gad he had known about the trysts there, but had chosen not to denounce Gad. With tears streaming down his face, Heinz revealed that the Nazis had forbidden him to wear his Nazi uniform. Because of his hump, he was a "defective" – not a shining example of Aryan masculinity. Heinz asked if he could help Gad and his friends, and he made his sexual interest in Gad abundantly clear. Heinz became a messenger for Gad and those in the underground.

Gad went into hiding and became part of a group that was known as *Chug Chaluzi* (Circle of Pioneers). Founded in 1943, the illegal youth group supported Jews in hiding. Group members helped each other obtain food, false ID cards, and places to stay. Gad and others in the group survived on wit, courage, charm, and luck. The group also depended on wealthy or well-connected patrons who could do them favors, and who often expected favors in return. One of Gad's benefactors was a wealthy engineer named Paul Dreyer. He found Gad a place to stay and always brought bread or meat or some other food when he came calling. No living arrangement was secure, but Gad stayed hidden in a variety of locations and survived until 1945. Then his luck ran out. He was arrested by the SS and thrown into prison in the last few weeks of the war, just before the Germans surrendered.

LEFT: Manfred's gift to Gad on their parting was his notebook. Gad kept it for the rest of his life.

Many who had helped him were also arrested in a major round-up. Paul Dreyer was arrested and accused of treason for aiding and abetting Jews. In his defense Dreyer said that he didn't know he was helping Jews – he had merely given the young men food because they were such attractive boys. It made no difference. The interrogators realized Dreyer was a homosexual. They set their specially trained dogs on him. Gad was much more fortunate; he was only imprisoned and repeatedly interrogated. He survived and was liberated when the Allies arrived in Berlin.

CHAPTER 8
Aftermath

At the end of the war, in 1945, the Allied forces entered the concentration camps, where they discovered horrific conditions. Those who had managed to survive were near death. For many homosexual prisoners, their ordeal was not over.

In reality, the Allied forces had limited sympathy for homosexual prisoners. They came from countries such as Canada, England, the United States, and Russia where homosexuality was still illegal. So if the men had served out the term of their original sentence, they were most likely freed, but if there was time left on their prison term, then they were kept incarcerated to serve out the balance of their sentences.

Homosexuals who eventually were allowed to return home found that the stigma of having been a pink triangle prisoner, or a "175er," or of having been arrested as a criminal homosexual, made regaining a normal existence extremely difficult. When Pierre Seel wrote his memoir, he had originally called it *Liberation Was for Others,* referring to the challenges he had finding any sort of normal life after being in a concentration camp.

Many in the years after the war didn't even consider homosexual prisoners as victims – they viewed the survivors as men with a criminal past. Nor did young gay men growing up after the war look to the gay victims of the Holocaust as role models. Canadian Peter Brattke remembers growing up in Germany and knowing that one of the men where he worked had been in a concentration camp because he was a homosexual. Peter made sure not to be seen even talking to him; the man's past made him an object of ridicule and scorn.

Homosexuality remained a punishable offense throughout Germany after the war. In West Germany the Nazi version of Paragraph 175 remained law until 1969. East Germany maintained a less strict version of Paragraph 175 until 1968. Between 1949 and 1969 more than 100,000 men were arrested for homosexuality in West Germany. Many of these men were sentenced to years in prison. Those who previously had been held in concentration camps as pink triangles were treated harshly, since they were considered repeat offenders.

Even with the murder of Ernst Röhm and the execution of other Nazi homosexuals, at the end of the war there was still the lingering belief that the SS was rife with homosexuals. There was little proof of this accusation, but it was another way of showing disgust for the Nazi

Party. Unfortunately, these rumors of homosexuality in the Nazi Party revealed the continuing disdain for homosexuality in general.

▼

It was the revolutionary period of the 1960s that brought change to Europe and North America. The year 1969 was extremely important for gay liberation. In Germany the Nazi-era laws criminalizing homosexuality were abolished, and in the United States on June 28, 1969, customers at a popular New York gay bar called the Stonewall Inn became angry at being harassed by the police. They took a stand that led to demonstrations in support of gay rights throughout the city and throughout the world. Gay men and lesbians were no longer willing to be treated as second-class citizens. They looked to the future for greater freedom and demanded recognition for their suffering in the past.

But for those who had worn the pink triangle, liberation was still a dream.

Very few homosexuals who had suffered during the Nazi era were willing to tell their stories. They were more interested in living their lives than revisiting horrors that had befallen them twenty and thirty years earlier. Returning home from the camps, they had been treated as ordinary criminals. They were not able to work in the civil service, lost their academic and professional degrees, and were unable to vote. But they were the lucky men arrested under Paragraph 175 – they were still alive.

It was after the 1972 publication of Josef Kohout's book, *The Men with the Pink Triangle* (written under the name Heinz Heger), and after the international success of *Bent* (the play based on the book) that people began to comprehend the horror of the Nazi persecution of homosexual men.

▼

The German and other European governments had established programs to assist victims of the Nazi regime. They were eligible to receive some compensation for the losses they had suffered. However, these programs did not include homosexuals because they were considered to be criminals. Men who had spent years in the concentration camps, had suffered unbelievable torture, had barely survived, and who would carry the scars of these horrific experiences for the rest of their lives, were denied any compensation.

Josef Kohout, who had struggled in Austria for recognition as a Nazi victim, discovered that the time he spent in the concentration camps would not be counted as years toward his government pension. He was infuriated to learn that Nazi guards (unless they were guilty of crimes against humanity) had no reduction to their pensions. Homosexual victims were being punished once again. Kohout fought back. But it was not until 1992 – forty-seven years later – that he won his fight and received his full pension. He was the only homosexual whose time in the camps was included in the calculation of his retirement pension.

Finally, in 2001, the German government recognized gays as victims of the Nazi regime. Homosexual survivors were encouraged to come forward and claim compensation for their treatment. By then, most of the men were either very elderly or dead.

CHAPTER 9
Recognition at Last

The horrors of Hitler's "Final Solution" and the slaughter of six million Jews were well documented. Jewish survivors of the Holocaust were encouraged to bear witness. Shortly after the war, monuments and days of remembrance were established to ensure that the world would not forget what had happened to Jews under Nazi rule. It took almost forty years for the first plaque acknowledging the suffering of gay men as victims of the Nazis to be erected.

The gay community was not even allowed to participate in the memorial services held at concentration camps or at war memorials. In 1970 gay activists in Amsterdam arrived at the National War Memorial in Dam Square with a lavender wreath to honor the gay men who had perished. The activists were arrested, and the wreath was removed and denounced as a disgrace.

In the 1980s, mounting pressure from activists, a greater awareness of the plight of homosexuals during the Nazi period, and a more tolerant attitude toward the gay community in general resulted in the first memorials to homosexual victims. In 1984 an official monument was unveiled at the former concentration camp at Mauthausen, Austria. A plaque in the shape of a pink triangle was mounted on the prison walls with the wording, "Put to death, Put to silence – for the homosexual victims of National Socialism."

In Dachau in 1985, another pink triangle plaque was displayed at the former concentration camp. A memorial sculpture made up of triangles of many different colors had been previously created in the camp, but had excluded the pink triangle. In 1990, at Buchenwald, a plaque appeared stating, "In memory of the homosexual men that suffered here. There were 650 *Rosa Winkel* (pink triangle) prisoners in the Buchenwald concentration camp between 1937 – 1945. Many of them lost their lives."

The gay community in Amsterdam was persistent in its demands for recognition of the suffering of homosexuals during the war. In 1987, seventeen years after the arrests at the National War Memorial, the Homomonument was opened. Close to the Anne Frank house, the monument is meant to "inspire and support gays in their struggle against denial, oppression, and discrimination." It is one of the largest monuments in the world honoring gay men and women.

In 1989 in Berlin, in the part of the city that housed many of the gay bars and clubs, including the famous Eldorado (which is once again a thriving gay club), a pink granite plaque in the shape of a triangle was placed outside the Nollendorfplatz subway station stating: "Killed and forgotten, the homosexual victims of National Socialism."

In Sydney, Australia, in San Francisco and Alaska in the United States, in both Rome and Trieste in Italy, in Montevideo, Uruguay, and, most recently, in Barcelona, Spain, monuments have been erected to remember the homosexuals who were victims of the Nazi regime. They make people consider the past, and encourage greater understanding of sexual diversity and the dignity of gay men and women.

Amsterdam's impressive monument honoring homosexual men and women is one of the world's largest.

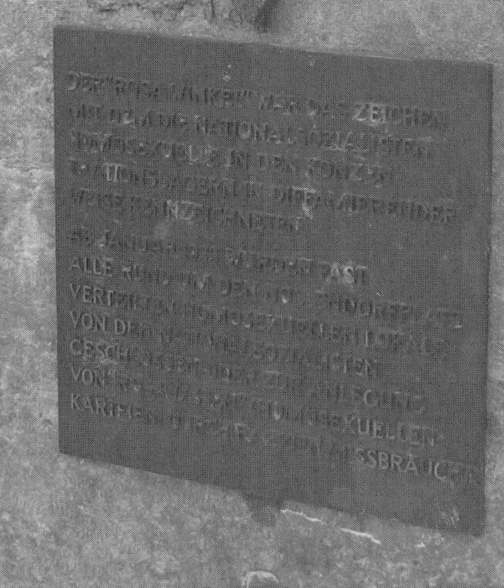
TOTGESCHLAGEN
TOTGESCHWIEGEN
DEN
HOMOSEXUELLEN OPFERN
DES
NATIONALSCZIALISMUS

In 2008, the Memorial to Homosexuals Persecuted under Nazism was unveiled in Berlin, across the street from the Memorial to the Murdered Jews of Europe. Visitors to the monument look inside a small window to watch two alternating videos: either two young men kissing or two women kissing. It is a monument distinctly different from others.

The video and the monument act as a strong reminder that these two young men certainly would have been arrested and would possibly have died if they had lived during the Nazi period. The wording on a nearby plaque concludes:

> Because of its history, Germany has a special responsibility to actively oppose the violation of gay men's and lesbians' human rights. In many parts of the world, people continue to be persecuted for their sexuality; homosexual love remains illegal and a kiss can be dangerous.
>
> With this memorial, the Federal Republic of Germany intends to honor the victims of persecution and murder, to keep alive the memory of this injustice, and to create a lasting symbol of opposition to enmity, intolerance, and the exclusion of gay men and lesbians.

LEFT: Berlin's pink granite tribute is outside a subway station in the area of the city where gay culture was celebrated in the years before the rise of the Nazi regime.

Even in the bleakest weather people come to view the video in the monument.

CHAPTER 10
The Survivors

What happened after the war to the persecuted and tortured young men you have met in this book? Not every story has a happy ending, but each of their stories deserves to be told and remembered.

Gad Beck

Gad Beck was still a young man at the end of the war. Eventually he made his way to Palestine, anxious to assist in establishment of the State of Israel. In 1995 he wrote his memoirs, *An Underground Life: Memoirs of a Gay Jew in Nazi Berlin*. Gad Beck died on June 14, 2012, and was thought to be the last of the homosexuals who suffered through the Nazi period in Germany.

Rudolf Brazda

When free, Rudolf went to the Alsace region in France. His skills as a roofer again provided him with a job. A few years later, while attending a costume ball, he met Edouard, the man who would be his companion for much of the rest of his life. Edouard was eighteen years younger than Rudolf. He was a Yugoslavian who had been kicked out of Yugoslavia and needed a new home. The two men discovered that they were very good for each other. Edouard and Rudolf lived together until Edouard's death in 2002.

Rudolf Brazda

In 2008 Rudolf Brazda came forward after seeing a German television program about a memorial to homosexual victims of Nazism in Berlin. He decided to tell his story. He spoke out about his experiences with the Nazis and his incarceration in Buchenwald, which had happened sixty-five years earlier. He was considered to be the last surviving man who had worn the pink triangle in a Nazi concentration camp. After living a rather quiet and anonymous life, Brazda became a symbol of gay pride and remembrance. His story resonated across Europe. He attended the gay pride march in Berlin shortly after the unveiling of Germany's gay Holocaust memorial, and went on to participate in events in many European cities, telling his story with the hope that young people would have a better understanding of the past. Shortly before his death in 2011, Rudolf Brazda was named a knight in France's Legion of Honor by President Nicolas Sarkozy.

Peter Flinsch

At the war's end Flinsch and his family were living in East Germany, and Peter used his talent as an artist to find work. His opportunities to draw and sketch had been extremely limited during the war. Now his artistic talent provided food and cigarettes when he painted large portraits of Lenin, Stalin, and Marx to hang outside public buildings. Through his art, he found work as a theatrical designer and as an illustrator and caricaturist for periodicals. In 1945 he met a bisexual actress, Gabriele Hessman, who was from West Germany. The two were married, giving Peter the opportunity to travel to the western zone of Berlin. It was there that he fell in love with his male friend Heino Heiden. In the early 1950s Peter moved to Canada to be with him. At first he worked designing scenery and sets for the Vancouver Ballet, but then the two men moved to Montreal where Peter began his career as designer and art director for the newly formed television division of the Canadian Broadcasting Corporation. By 1985, when he left the CBC, he had

Peter Flinsch in his studio in Canada.

won numerous awards for his work. But it was after retirement that he devoted himself to his own work and held many exhibitions of his art, which frequently depicts the male body. In, *Peter Flinsch: The Body in Question*, by Ross Higgins, Peter said, "I've seen many changes in my life, from incarceration to liberation. I hope I will see the day when the gay movement becomes just a part of the fabric of society." (1)

Peter Flinsch died in March 2010, one of the last remaining homosexual survivors of the Nazi regime.

Josef Kohout

Josef Kohout is known today for his 1972 book, *The Men with the Pink Triangle,* which he wrote under the name Heinz Heger. The book, now translated into many languages, was the first to document for the general public the suffering of homosexual prisoners in the Nazi concentration camps. The shame of homosexuality had barred gay men from writing about their experiences. Kohout's book opened the door for others to speak out. His book ends with these words:

Scarcely a word has been written on the fact that along with the millions whom Hitler had butchered on grounds of "race," hundreds of thousands of people were sadistically tortured to death simply for having homosexual feelings. Scarcely anyone has publicised the fact that the madness of Hitler and his gang was not directed just against the Jews, but also against us homosexuals, in both cases leading to the "final solution" of seeking the total annihilation of these human beings.

May they never be forgotten,
These multitudes of dead,
Our anonymous, immortal martyrs. [2]

Josef Kohout's story inspired playwright Martin Sherman to write the widely acclaimed play *Bent,* which opened in London in 1979 starring Ian McKellen and then in New York with Richard Gere. The success of the play encouraged the making of a film of the same name in 1997.

Josef never received any compensation after the war. He died in Vienna in 1994.

Stefan Kosinski

At the end of the war Stefan lived in a German displaced persons camp until 1947, when he was able to return to Poland. He suffered ill health for much of his life due to his imprisonment, and he never received any

Stefan Kosinski giving his testimony in 1995.

compensation for his suffering. Stefan never did find out what happened to Willi. He was terrified that his letter had delivered Willi to the Nazis and was afraid that if he went to Vienna, to Willi's family's house, he would bring only more difficulties to his first great love, or to his memory.

Stefan Kosinski told his story to writer Lutz Van Dijk, who wrote the book *Damned Strong Love: The True Story of Willi G. and Stefan K.* While working on the book in the late 1980s, Stefan started a systematic search for Willi, but his search through the Polish, Austrian, and German archives was unsuccessful. In 1994 he wrote, "To this day I have Willi to thank for my being able to experience feelings of love as something beautiful from the very beginning." (3)

In 1995, Stefan gave his testimony to the University of Southern California's Shoah Foundation Institute, as one of the homosexual survivors of Nazi persecution. He says on the video, "I wanted to show the world how I suffered for nothing.... For what? I didn't kill. I didn't steal. I did nothing wrong." (4) Willi's fate is still unknown.

Pierre Seel

Pierre survived the war, but like the other gay men who survived the concentration camps, he was not really liberated. He kept secret the burden of his homosexuality. He didn't tell his story due to shame and fear of further troubles. Homosexuality was still against the law in France. Seel decided to marry, and he fathered three children. He led a troubled life and had many marital and psychological problems. He discovered that living a lie and denying his homosexuality was extremely difficult. He spent many years battling depression and alcoholism.

In 1981, after Kohout's book, *The Men with the Pink Triangle*, was published, Seel decided to tell his story. He was the first French citizen to speak openly about his experience as a gay man sent to a concentration camp. Ultimately, he embraced his homosexuality and in 1994 wrote the book *I, Pierre Seel, Deported Homosexual: A Memoir of Nazi Terror (Moi, Pierre Seel, déporté homosexual)*. He dedicated his book to "my friend Jo, murdered in 1941. And to all the victims of the Nazi barbarity." (5)

Pierre Seel spent the last years of his life campaigning for recognition of homosexual victims of the Holocaust. When it was finally agreed in the 1990s that he might be due reparations, he was told that he would have to produce documentation. The official records could not be found to prove his internment. He was told to produce two affidavits from eyewitnesses. This proved to be an impossible task since most eyewitnesses had already died from old age. (Pierre Seel was one of the youngest men in the camp.)

By the end of the 1990s, when the filmmakers Rob Epstein and

Three years after Pierre Seel's death in 2005, his adopted city of Toulouse, France, named a street in his honor.

Jeffrey Friedman were capturing the experiences of gays imprisoned or affected by the Nazis for their documentary film *Paragraph 175*, they wanted to interview Seel for the film. Klaus Müller, a gay historian from Germany, was the interviewer. At first, Pierre was reluctant to do the interview, since he had sworn that he would never shake hands with a German again, but his attitude softened when he realized this young gay historian was fighting for reparations for homosexual victims. Pierre still had trouble revisiting the horrors of those years. He tried to explain to Müller, "It's difficult to talk about that time. I am ninety percent disabled from the war.... Do you think I can talk about that? That it is good for me? This is too much for my nerves. I can't do this anymore. I am ashamed for humanity. Ashamed." (6)

Pierre Seel died in 2005; he never knew that in Toulouse a street was renamed in his honor. There, a plaque reads, "Rue Pierre Seel – Déporté français pour homosexualité – 1923-2005."

▼

No one knows how many homosexuals did not survive the Nazi regime.

The number of gay men murdered in the concentration camps is not known, the number of men in the army who were executed for homosexuality is not known, and the number of Jewish men who were homosexuals and sent to the gas chambers is unknown as well. In addition to those who died at the hands of the Nazis, it is impossible to know how many men took their own lives rather than be arrested as homosexuals. The exact numbers are not really the point. What is crucial is remembering that thousands of men died because of their homosexuality.

Many of their stories have been lost.

For some, all that remains are their pictures, taken at the time of their arrest. For many others, even their names have been lost. We must not forget them.

CONCLUSION

It Gets Better

In 2011, in response to the suicides of gay teens, a video campaign was launched in the United States by author and journalist Dan Savage and his husband, Terry Miller. Known as *It Gets Better*, the campaign was created to support lesbian, gay, bisexual, and transgender (LGBT) youth in the United States. It quickly became international, with supporters flooding in from around world. The campaign has been supported by celebrities – including Ellen DeGeneres, Neil Patrick Harris, and English rugby star Ben Cohen – and by international leaders – such as Desmond Tutu in South Africa and British Prime Minister David Cameron – all of whom have recorded videos and messages of support. The Royal Canadian Mounted Police released a video with their staff sharing experiences of being gay men and women in the force and ensuring viewers that it gets better.

Each of us is encouraged to pledge the following:

> Everyone deserves to be respected for who they are. I pledge to spread this message to my friends, family, and neighbors. I'll speak up against hate and intolerance whenever I see it, at school and at work. I'll provide hope for lesbian, gay, bi, trans, and other bullied teens by letting them know that "It Gets Better."

Fifty years ago, let alone one hundred years ago, this pledge couldn't have been imagined. Immense changes have occurred in the attitudes toward gays. *It has gotten better* – not just for gay youth facing the challenges of adolescence, but also for the LGBT community at large. Never before has there been the same degree of acceptance, tolerance, and respect for the LGBT community.

That is not to say that there isn't still bullying and hatred toward the LGBT community by individuals and some groups, but there is more support for LGBT youth than there has ever been in the past. There is a fight to stop bullying against members of the LGBT community in person and in cyberspace.

On December 15, 2011, the United Nations released the first-ever report on the human rights of LGBT people. The chilling report details how around the world people are killed or endure hate-motivated violence, torture, detention, criminalization, and discrimination in jobs, health care, and education because of their real or perceived sexual orientation or gender identity. In the report, the UN High Commissioner for Human Rights calls on countries to repeal laws that criminalize homosexuality, abolish the death penalty for offenses involving consensual sexual relations, harmonize the age of consent for heterosexual and homosexual conduct, and enact comprehensive anti-discrimination laws. The report stresses the need to champion the LGBT community and highlights the great strides that have been made in the last two decades with thirty countries decriminalizing homosexuality.

The report identifies the seventy-six countries in the world where it remains illegal to engage in same-sex conduct. In at least five countries – Iran, Mauritania, Saudi Arabia, Sudan, and Yemen – a conviction can result in the death penalty.

While homosexuality is still outlawed and punishable by law in some places, there are a growing number of other places where same-sex marriages are legal. Gay pride is honored in cities such as Amsterdam, Barcelona, Berlin, Buenos Aires, Copenhagen, London, Mexico City, New York, Paris, San Francisco, Shanghai, Sydney, Tel Aviv, and Toronto. These cities embrace gay culture and have large, vibrant gay communities. The colorful rainbow flag is used to identify the LGBT communities, and the color pink is used to celebrate gay culture. In Toronto the directory of gay businesses is called *The Pink Pages*; in France the LGBT television station is called *Pink TV;* and in Britain gay news is delivered through the *Pink News*. Businesses actively seek out "pink" dollars – the money spent within the LGBT community, also known as the *Pink Economy*.

Why pink?

Because pink was the color of persecution for gay men in Nazi Germany. It is forever linked to the pink triangle they were forced to wear in concentration camps to identify themselves as homosexuals. The color pink comes from a bleak and terrifying period of gay history, but today it is a color of remembrance and celebration.

▼

True to her word, Kitty Fischer never did forget the man who had pulled her out of the latrine at Auschwitz. And she never forgot the story he told her. He was forced to wear the pink triangle because he was a homosexual – he lived with another man. When he had arrived at Auschwitz, the Nazis asked him how he made his living. They laughed when he told them he was a portrait painter and said they had the perfect job for him. They gave him a brush and a bucket of whitewash, and for seven days a week, ten hours a day, he used his skill to brush the filth off the latrines. That's how he came to witness Kitty's humiliation.

By the time Kitty and her sister had arrived at the camp, the war was not going well for the Germans. Camps were being closed, and evidence of the atrocities that had taken place in them was being destroyed. When the man with the pink triangle learned he was being sent to dismantle another camp, he feared the girls would be killed if they stayed in Auschwitz. He told Kitty that some women were to be sent out of the camp to work in a weaving factory and that they must find a way to be part of the group.

Only fifty women were chosen, but Kitty and her sister were among them, after Kitty made up a story that her family had owned a weaving factory in Czechoslovakia. She never saw the man with the pink triangle again. She never even knew his name. She only knew that he had saved their lives and that she would never forget him.

Many years later, in 2001, when the Gay and Lesbian Holocaust Memorial Park was dedicated in Sydney, Australia, where Kitty then lived, she said, "I don't know what happened to him, but I made a promise that if I ever got out of Auschwitz alive, I would tell the story of the pink triangle man who brought me two jacket potatoes every day and saved my and my sister's lives." (1)

The memorial was Kitty's brainchild, and she played a major role in its fundraising. Those who visit the Gay and Lesbian Memorial Park opposite Sydney's Jewish Museum can read the inscription:

We remember you who have suffered or died
at the hands of others.
Women who have loved women,
Men who have loved men;
And all those who have refused
the roles others
have expected us to play.
Nothing shall purge
your deaths from our
memories.

Afterword

In the fall of 2010 and the fall of 2011, I traveled to Europe to visit some of the sites discussed in this book. As a gay man born in the 1950s, and having lived through the sexual revolution, I found it hard to comprehend the horrors suffered by men simply because of their sexuality.

Visiting the former concentration camp at Sachsenhausen on a bitterly cold day was frightening. I was dressed for winter, and yet I was suffering from the freezing temperatures. The feeling of death seemed to permeate the camp. My winter boots, hat, and gloves protected me, but I knew that the men who had been housed in the camp wore little more than their uniforms, with virtually no protection from the cold. I knew that on cold days some men were sent naked and wet to stand in the freezing temperatures. Their suffering could only be imagined.

When I saw the gas chamber, it was sobering to realize that thousands of bodies had been cremated there. But it was when I saw the poles used to suspend men by their wrists tied behind them that I was well and truly horrified. The idea that men could inflict such punishment on other men made the day so much bleaker.

Writing this book has given me the opportunity to think about my own privileges, and that I was able to grow up relatively unscarred by my preference for my own sex. While I take comfort in realizing that gays and lesbians are no longer persecuted the way they once were in Europe, I am also more aware of the torments that await gay men and women in the less enlightened countries of the world. The fight for gays to live a normal life persists. I truly hope that it continues to get better for gay youth everywhere.

Acknowledgments

This book would not have been possible without the help of a great many people. First I have to thank Margie Wolfe for suggesting the topic. It is heartening to know that a feminist press is anxious to broaden the discussion of the victims of the Holocaust to include the men branded with a pink triangle. To Margie, Carolyn Jackson, and Emma Rodgers at Second Story Press I offer my sincere thanks. It was a great honor for me to have Malcolm Lester begin the editing process for this book. For me, having known and admired Malcolm for many years, it was a career highlight to have him on this project.

I have worked as a librarian for more than thirty years and writing this book highlighted just how important librarians can be. The staff at the Toronto Public Library was extremely helpful when I needed to find information. It is the international librarians that I met through my research I would truly like to thank. On a visit to Amsterdam I was fortunate to receive assistance from Connie Van Gies. Her desire to help a foreign researcher was inspiring. In Berlin, Dr. Jens Dobler of the Schwules Museum offered invaluable help. Finally, in Washington D. C. at the United States Holocaust Memorial Museum I had the tremendous good fortune to meet librarian Ron Coleman and archivist Caroline Wadell who guided me to stories and photos that helped make this book much richer.

On a personal note I give tremendous thanks to my partner Martin Fichman. Nobody has read or heard the stories in this book more than he has. I owe him a huge debt. A dear friend, Jan Bartelli, journeyed to Germany with us while I was researching the treatment of gay men during the Holocaust. I will always remember the brutally cold day on which we trudged through the snow at Sachsenhausen. Jan made a difficult trip a much more pleasant one. When I first embarked on this project I went to Peter Brattke who grew up in post-war Germany. His advice and perspective were a great help.

I would also like to thank early readers of the book, Barbara Egerer, Greg Kroetsch, and Graeme Leslie. Their honest responses were truly appreciated. Thanks also to Lenore Lucey for being such a gracious host while I was doing research in Washington.

Finally, I would like to thank my sister, Wendy Setterington, who wrote an essay on why Anne Frank was her hero. It was published in *The Globe and Mail* when she was in grade four. At the time, I was in grade two and she inspired me – she still does.

APPENDIX

Timeline of Events Crucial for Homosexual Men in Germany

1871	German Penal Code includes Paragraph 175, criminalizing sexual acts between men.
1897	Dr. Magnus Hirschfeld establishes Berlin's Scientific-Humanitarian Committee – the first worldwide homosexual rights organization.
1898	Hirschfeld attempts to repeal Paragraph 175.

1919	First gay themed movie released in Germany – *Different from the Others* – pushes for the repeal of Paragraph 175. Hirschfeld establishes the Institute for Sexual Research.
1921	Adolf Hitler becomes leader of the Nazi Party.
1928	Hitler declares, "Anyone who thinks of homosexual love is our enemy."
1930	Nazi leader Ernst Röhm becomes leader of the SA (Storm Troopers).
1931	Röhm's homosexuality questioned in the media.
1933	**JANUARY 30** Nazis gain power in Germany. Adolf Hitler sworn in as Chancellor. **FEBRUARY 23** Gay and lesbian bars and journals are forbidden in directives on "Public Morality." **FEBRUARY 28** Hitler is made *Führer* (leader) of Germany.

	MARCH Nazis open Dachau concentration camp near Munich. **MARCH 5** Eldorado Club in Berlin closed (large homosexual clientele). **MAY 6** Nazis destroy Hirschfeld's Institute for Sexual Research. **MAY 10** Nazi hold large book burnings, including burning the thousands of books held in the Institute founded by Hirschfeld. Throughout 1933, criminal proceedings against homosexual men rise.
1934	**JUNE 30 - JULY 2** Night of the Long Knives – Hitler has Röhm murdered along with the other leaders of the SA. Treachery is cited as the reason, and his homosexuality is used as additional justification. Himmler made head of the SS and gains control of the SA and all concentration camps.

1935	**JUNE 28** Ministry of Justice revises Paragraph 175. Revision provides the legal basis for extending the Nazi persecution of homosexuals. Any act that could be construed as homosexual, "criminally indecent activities between men," is punishable. Law broadened – now even an embrace between men is punishable. **SEPTEMBER 15** Nuremberg Laws – The Laws for the Protection of German Blood and German Honor – passed. Deprives German Jews of citizenship and rights. Magnus Hirschfeld dies in France.
1936	Olympics held in Berlin – some gay bars reopened and some anti-Semitic signs are removed. **OCTOBER 26** Himmler forms the Reich Central Office for Combating Abortion and Homosexuality. In show trials against independent youth groups and the Catholic church, the Nazis use homophobia as a tool of denunciation.

	Sachsenhausen concentration camp opens near Berlin – men arrested under the revised Paragraph 175 sent there and to similar camps being established. Himmler orders that any SS men caught in homosexual acts are to be put in concentration camps and then shot while trying to "escape." Roma, Sinti, and Jehovah's Witnesses are arrested and sent to concentration camps.
1937 - 1939	Peak years of homosexual persecution.
1938	**APRIL 4** Gestapo directive – men convicted of homosexuality will be incarcerated in concentration camps. **NOVEMBER 7** Killing of Ernst vom Rath (a German diplomat in Paris and a suspected homosexual) by seventeen-year-old Jewish youth Herschel Grynszpan provides pretext for Kristallnacht.

	NOVEMBER 9 Kristallnacht – looting and destroying of Jewish property, beating and killing of Jews, and the arrest and internment of 20,000 Jewish men. Kristallnacht marks the beginning of the Nazi's efforts to eliminate the Jews.
1939	**SEPTEMBER 1** Poland invaded – beginning of the Second World War. Austrian men convicted for homosexual offenses are deported to Mauthausen concentration camp. **OCTOBER** Hitler initiates a decree empowering physicians to grant a "mercy" death to the mentally and physically challenged, or any person considered to be genetically defective.
1940	The deportation of German Jews to Poland commences. **JULY 12** Himmler decrees that homosexuals (who have seduced more than one partner), after finishing their prison term, will be sent to concentration camps for preventive detention.

1941	**NOVEMBER 15** Hitler orders death penalty for any SS officer engaged in homosexual behavior.
1942	The mass gassing of Jews begins in the death camps in occupied Poland – millions are murdered.
1944	Hitler occupies Germany's former ally Hungary. The Nazis send 476,000 Hungarian Jews to Auschwitz.
1945	**MAY** End of war. Russians liberate Auschwitz, the British liberate Bergen-Belsen, and the Americans liberate Dachau. Hitler commits suicide in his Berlin bunker. **OCTOBER** Beginning of the Nuremberg trials – Nazi persecution of homosexuals not addressed.
1950 - 1951	East Germany replaces the 1935 Nazi version of Paragraph 175 with the 1871 version. West Germany keeps the Nazi version in place.
1950s - 60s	Thousands of homosexuals are imprisoned in West Germany under the Nazi version of Paragraph 175.

1968	Paragraph 175 is liberalized in East Germany – homosexual acts between consenting adults are no longer criminalized.
1969	Paragraph 175 revised in West Germany
1973	Further revisions to Paragraph 175
1984	First commemorative plaque acknowledging homosexual prisoners installed in Mauthausen concentration camp.
1985	West German President Richard von Weizsäcker includes first public acknowledgement of homosexual persecution at the 40th anniversary of the end of the Second World War. Plaques installed at Dachau and Neuengamme concentration camps acknowledging the suffering of homosexual prisoners.
1987	Monument to the persecution of homosexuals erected in Amsterdam.
1989	Plaque installed in Berlin's Nollendorfplatz area commemorating the persecution of gays (close to the Eldorado club – closed in 1933).

1994	Homosexual acts removed from legislation in Germany.
2001	Sydney, Australia - memorial erected to mark the persecution of homosexuals. German government formally apologizes to homosexual victims of the Nazis. Survivors have to the end of 2001 to come forward for restitution.
2008	**MAY 27** Monument unveiled in Berlin dedicated to the homosexuals persecuted by the Nazis.
2011	**AUGUST 3** Rudolf Brazda, last known gay man to have survived being sent to a concentration camp, dies.
2012	**JUNE 14** Gad Beck, last known gay Jewish survivor, dies.

Bibliography

Bartoletti, Susan Campbell, *Hitler Youth: Growing Up in Hitler's Shadow.* Scholastic Inc., New York, 2005.

Beck, Gad, *An Underground Life: Memoirs of a Gay Jew in Nazi Berlin.* Written with Frank Heibert. The University of Wisconsin Press, Madison, 1999. Translated from the German by Allison Brown.

Dijk, Lutz van, *Damned Strong Love: The True Story of Willi G. And Stephan K.* Henry Holt and Company, New York, 1995. Translated from the German by Elizabeth D. Crawford.

Epstein, Rob, and Jeffrey Freedman, *Paragraph 175* (DVD). New Yorker Films, New York, 2000.

Giles, Geoffrey J., "The Institutionalization of Homosexual Panic in the Third Reich" in *Social Outsiders in Nazi Germany.* Edited by Robert Gellately and Nathan Stoltzfus. Princeton University Press, Princeton and Oxford, 2001.

Heger, Heinz, *The Men with the Pink Triangle.* Alyson Publications, Boston, 1980. English translation by David Fernbach.

Higgins, Ross, *Peter Flinsch: The Body in Question.* Arsenal Pulp Press, Vancouver, 2008.

Isherwood, Christopher, *Goodbye to Berlin.* Hogarth Press, London, 1939.

———, *Christopher and His Kind.* North Point Press, New York, 1996.

Mathias, Sean, *Bent* (DVD). MGM Home Entertainment, Los Angeles, 2003.

Morsch, Gunter, and Astrid Ley (eds.), *Sachsenhausen Concentration Camp:1936–1945 Events and Developments.* Metropol Verlag, Berlin, 2010.

Müller, Klaus, *Who Can I Trust? Homosexuals during the Nazi Era.* Verzetsmuseum, Amsterdam, 2006. English Translation by Marieke Piggott.

Plant, Richard, *The Pink Triangle: The Nazi War Against Homosexuals.* A New Republic Book, Henry Holt and Company, New York, 1986.

Reinfelder, Monika (ed.), *Amazon to Zami: Towards Global Feminism.* Cassell, London, 1996.

Schoppmann, Claudia, *Days of Masquerade: Life Stories of Lesbians during the Third Reich.* Columbia University Press, New York, 1996. English translation by Allison Brown.

Seel, Pierre, *I Pierre Seel, Deported Homosexual: A Memoir of Nazi Terror.* Basic Books, a Division of HarperCollins Publishers, Inc., New York, 1995. English translation by Joachim Neugroschel.

Sherman, Martin, *Bent.* Samuel French, New York, 1979.

Sternweiler, Andre, *Self-Confidence and Persistence: Two Hundred Years of History.* Schwules Museum, Berlin, 2008.

Tamagne, Florence, *A History of Homosexuality in Europe: Berlin, London, Paris 1919 –1939.* Algora Publishing, New York, 2006.

Notes

Chapter 1
Berlin - Homosexual Capital of the World

1. During this period, "homosexuals" referred specifically to men. The word "gay" was not in common use.
2. Epstein, Rob, and Jeffrey Freedman, *Paragraph 175*, DVD, section on F. Heinz

Chapter 2
The Rise of the Nazis

1. Hitler, Adolf, *Mein Kampf*, p.66
2. Reich Ministry of the Interior, *Reichgesetzblatt*, Part I, 1935 (United States Holocaust Museum Collection)

3. Plant, Richard, *The Pink Triangle*, p.49
4. Plant, Richard, *The Pink Triangle*, p.50
5. Becker, Albrecht, *Paragraph 175*, DVD
6. Plant, Richard, *The Pink Triangle*, p.61
7. Plant, Richard, *The Pink Triangle*, p.63
8. The History Place, 2001 www.historyplace.com

Chapter 3
The Gay Life Is Over

1. London *Telegraph*, 4 August 2011, "The Last of the Pink Triangles Tells his Story"
2. Interview with Brazda, YouTube, http://www.youtube.com/watch?v=x1uFsOXWhQ&noredirect
3. Schoppmann, Claudia, *Days of Masquerade: Life stories of Lesbians during the Third Reich*, 1996, p.97
4. Higgins, Ross, *Peter Flinsch: The Body in Question,* p.13
5. Higgins, Ross, *Peter Flinsch: The Body in Question,* p.13
6. Hays, Mathew, "Montreal Artist Felt Free to be Himself," *The Globe and Mail*, May 12, 2010
7. Higgins, Ross, *Peter Flinsch: The Body in Question,* p.18

Chapter 4
The Master Race –
The Nazi Plan to Rid Germany of the Inferior

1. *Simon Wiesenthal Center Annual,* Volume 7, 1990

2. Epstein, Rob, and Jeffrey Freedman, *Paragraph 175*, DVD
3. Plant, Richard, *The Men with the Pink Triangle,* p.111
4. Seel, Pierre, *I Pierre Seel, Deported Homosexual: A Memoir of Nazi Terror,* p.26
5. Seel, Pierre, *I Pierre Seel, Deported Homosexual: A Memoir of Nazi Terror,* p.38
6. Seel, Pierre, *I Pierre Seel, Deported Homosexual: A Memoir of Nazi Terror,* p.38
7. Müller, Klaus, *Who Can I Trust?* p.5
8. Müller, Klaus, *Who Can I Trust?* p.5

Chapter 5
Death through Work – Imprisonment in the Concentration Camps

1. Schoppmann, Claudia, *Days of Masquerade: Life Stories of Lesbians during the Third Reich*, p. 23
2. Epstein, Rob, and Jeffrey Freedman, Par*agraph 175*, DVD, section on Pierre Seel
3. Plant, Richard, *The Pink Triangle,* p. 163
4. Epstein, Rob, and Jeffrey Freedman, *Paragraph 175*, DVD, section on Dormer Heinz
5. Plant, Richard, *The Pink Triangle, p.175*
6. Heger, Heinz, *The Men with the Pink Triangle*, p.20
7. Heger, Heinz, *The Men with the Pink Triangle*, p.21
8. All of the quotes of Kohout's interrogation can be found in Heger,

Heinz, *The Men with the Pink Triangle*, p. 23
9. Heger, Heinz, *The Men with the Pink Triangle*, p.33
10. Heger, Heinz, *The Men with the Pink Triangle*, p.43

Chapter 6
Nazis in Occupied Territories

1. Dijk, Lutz van, *Damned Strong Love: The True Story of Willi G. and Stephan K.*, p. 83

Chapter 7
Jewish Homosexuals

1. Beck, Gad, *An Underground Life: Memoirs of a Gay Jew in Nazi Berlin* , p.22
2. Beck, Gad, *An Underground Life: Memoirs of a Gay Jew in Nazi Berlin,* p.55
3. Beck, Gad, *An Underground Life: Memoirs of a Gay Jew in Nazi Berlin,* p.69
4. Beck, Gad, *An Underground Life: Memoirs of a Gay Jew in Nazi Berlin,* p.70
5. Beck, Gad, *An Underground Life: Memoirs of a Gay Jew in Nazi Berlin,* p.70

Chapter 10
The Survivors

1. Higgins, Ross, *Peter Flinsch: The Body in Question*, p.53

2. Heger, Heinz, *The Men with the Pink Triangle*, p.115
3. Dijk, Lutz, *Damned Strong Love*, p.134
4. Shoah Foundation interview, University of Southern California Shoah Foundation Institute for visual history and education, 1995 http://dornsife.usc.edu/vhi/cms/?q=node/1544
5. Seel, Pierre, *I Pierre Seel, Deported Homosexual: A Memoir of Nazi Terror*, Dedication Page
6. Epstein, Rob, and Jeffrey Freedman, *Paragraph 175*, DVD, section on Pierre Seel

Conclusion
It Gets Better

1. Epstein, Rob, and Jeffrey Freedman, *Paragraph 175*, DVD, additional footage, interview with Kitty Fischer

Index

*italicized numbers denote photographs

**italicized numbers with *t* denote tables/charts

A

abortion, 11, 44, 126

Amsterdam, gay activism in, 97–99, *99, 100,* 115, 130

Anders als die Andern (Different from the Others), 7, *7*

Auschwitz, 1, 58, 73, 116–17, 129

Austria

  annexation to Third Reich, 83

  deportation of Austrian men convicted of homosexual offense, 128

  Hitler's plans to unite Germany and, 10

Hitler's policies for homosexuals in, 75
Josef Kohout's experience in, 64–67

B

Beck, Gad, 81–90, *82, 83, 85, 88,* 103, 131
Belzec, 58
Bent (book, play), 94, 107
Berlin
attacks against homosexuals in, 16–18, *17,* 30–31, 43
concentration camps near, 57
Gad Beck's and Jewish life during the war, in, 82–90
homosexual culture in prewar, 3–8, *4, 5, 6, 7,* 13, *16,* 17
memorials to victims of National Socialism in, 98–99, 101, *102,* 130, 131
mercy killings (Operation T) in, 38
Brazda, Rudolf, 25–30, *104,* 104–5, 131
brothels, as "cure" for homosexuality, 72–72
Brownshirts. *See* Storm Troopers
Buchenwald, 27–30, *28,* 57, 98, 104

C

Cabaret, 8
castration, 64, 72
Catholics, persecution of, 45–51, 64–73, 126
Chełmno, 58

Christopher and His Kind, 8
Chug Chaluzi (Circle of Pioneers), 89
compensation for gay victims, 94–95, 107–8
concentration camps. *See also* death camps
  Buchenwald, 27–30, 57, 98, 104
  Dachau, 16–17, 57, 98, 125, 129, 130
  Esterwegen, 57
  Flossenbürg, 57, 72–73
  Mauthausen, *49,* 57, 128, 130
  Natzweiler, 60–61
  Oranienburg, 57
  Ravensbrück, 57, 73
  Sachsenhausen, *56,* 61, 67–71, *71,* 119–20, 122, 127
  Schirmeck-Vorbruck, 60
concentration camps, mapped, *57*
Czechoslovakia, 10, 27, 57, 117

D
Dachau, 16–17, 57, 98, 125, 129, 130
Damned Strong Love: The True Story of Willi G. and Stephan K., 108
death camps. *See also* concentration camps
  Auschwitz, 1, 58, 73, 116–17, 129
  Belzec, 58
  Chełmno, 58
  Majdanek, 58

Sobibor, 58
Treblinka, 58
death camps mapped, *57*
death marches, 30, 80
death sentence for homosexual behavior, 52, 53
denunciation of homosexuals, 51–52
Der Eigene (His Own Self), 3
Die Freundin (The Girlfriend), 5
Die Insel (The Island), 3
"dolly boys," 61, 63
Dreyer, Paul, 89, 90

E
Einstein, Albert, 13
Eldorado (club), *16,* 17, *17,* 98–99
Epstein, Rob, 109–10
Esterwegen, 57
experiments, medical, 50, *63,* 63–64

F
Fischer, Kitty, 1–2, 116–17, *117*
Flinsch, Peter, 31–35, *32,* 105–6, *106*
Flossenbürg, 57, 72–73
France, 18, 45–48, 75, 109–10, 115
Frauenliebe (Women's Love), 5
Friedman, Jeffrey, 110

G
Gestapo, 41
directive regarding homosexuals, 52, 127
interrogation methods, 47–48, 66–67, 79
Goodbye to Berlin, 8
Göring, Hermann, 22
Grune, Richard, *62*
gypsies, 16. *See also* Roma

H
Hachshara, 84
Hesse, Hermann, 13
Heydrich, Reinhard, 22
Himmler, Heinrich, 16, 22, 40–44, *41,* 52–53, 125, 126, 127, 128
Hirschfeld, Dr. Magnus, 7–8, *11,* 11–14, 18, *18,* 123, 124, 125, 126
Hitler, Adolf. *See also* Nazi
anti-Semitism of, 10, 14
persecution of homosexuals, 97, 107, 129
plan to establish "master race," 25, 37–38, 75, 128
relationship to Röhm and the SA, 19–23
rise to power, 10, 15
supreme authority of, 25
timeline of events related to, 124, 125, 128, 129
homosexuality, criminalization of. *See* Paragraph 175

I

I, Pierre Seel, Deported Homosexual, 109
Institute for Sexual Research, *12*, 13, 17, 124, 125
Isherwood, Christopher, 8
It Gets Better (video campaign), 113–14

J

Jehovah's Witnesses, 16, 26, 45, 58, 127
Jews
  homosexual, 81–90, 103, 111
  persecution of, 45, 53, 55, 58, 81–90
  recognition of crimes against, 97, 101
  timeline of events related to, 126–29, 131

K

kapo, 29–30, 60–63, 71–72
Kohout, Josef, 64–73, *65*, 93, 94, 106–7
Kosinski, Stefan, 76–80, 107–8, *108*

L

Ledige Frauen (Single Women), 5
lesbians
  under National Socialism, 30–31, 52, 60, 81
  Nazi's position on, 14–16
  post-war period, 93, 101, 120
  pre-war culture, 5–7

Luftwaffe, 22, 33–35

M
Majdanek, 58
Mann, Thomas, 13
masturbation, 32–33, 61
Mauthausen, *49,* 57, 128, 130
medical experiments, 50, *63,* 63–64
Menschenrecht (Human Rights), 3, *5*
Men with the Pink Triangle, The, 106, 109
"mercy killings," 37–38, 128
Müller, Klaus, 110

N
Natzweiler, 60–61
Nazi
    concentration camps, 55–60
    persecution of homosexuals, 10, 14–19, *28,* 38–40, 42–45, *44t,* 51–53, *59,* 60–64, *68*
    persecution of Jews, 81–89
    plans for a master race, 25, 37–38, 75
    recognition of crimes by, 94–95, 97–102
    rise to power, 10, 15, 20–23
    timeline of events related to, 124–26, 128–29, 131
Night of the Long Knives, 22–23, 25, 125

O

Operation Hummingbird, 22. *See also* Night of the Long Knives
Oranienburg, 57

P

Paragraph 175
activists' attempts to abolish, 7, *11,* 11–13
early Nazi position on, 14–15
enforcement in occupied countries, 75
history of, 10
men arrested under, 58, 69–70
Nazi's 1935 revisions to, 38–40, *39t,* 45
post-war period, 92
timeline of events related to, 123–25, 127, 129, 130
Paragraph 175 (film), 110
pink lists, 43–44, 45, 47–48
Poland, 10, 58, 75, 76–80, 128, 129

R

racial "inferiority," 16, 37–38
racial purity, 15, 25, 37–38, 42–43, 75
Ravensbrück, 57, 73
Reichswehr, 21
Rembrandt, van Rijn, 32
Rilke, Rainer Maria, 13
Röhm, Ernst, 18–23, *19, 20,* 25, 40, 42–43, 92, 124, 125

Roma, 16, 55, 58, 73, 127

S

SA *(Sturmabteilung). see* Storm Troopers
Sachsenhausen, *56,* 61, 67–71, *71,* 119–20, 122, 127
Schirmeck-Vorbruck, 60
Schoppmann, Claudia, 60
Schutzhaft, 27
Seel, Pierre, 45–51, 92, 109–10, *110*
Sherman, Martin, 107
Sinti, 16, 37, 127. *See also* Roma
Sobibor, 58
SS *(Schutzstaffel)*, 16, 22
Stonewall Inn, 93
Storm Troopers, *19,* 20–23, 124, 125

T

Treaty of Versailles, 9, 10
Treblinka, 58

W

World War I, 9–10

Z

Zazou, 45–46, *46,* 48

Photo Credits

Page 4: © United States Holocaust Memorial Museum (USHMM)
Page 5: © USHMM
Page 6: all photos © USHMM
Page 7: © USHMM
Page 11: © USHMM
Page 12: © USHMM
Page 16: © USHMM
Page 17: © USHMM
Page 18: © USHMM
Page 19: © Bundesarchiv, Bild 102-14393 / photographer: Georg Pahl
Page 20: © USHMM

Page 28: © USHMM
Page 32: © Stuart Seeley
Page 41: all photos © USHMM
Page 46: public domain
Page 49: © USHMM
Page 56: @ Ken Setterington
Page 57: illustration by Jenny Watson
Page 59: © USHMM
Page 62: © Ken Setterington; © Schwules Museum Berlin
Page 63: © Ken Setterington
Page 65: © USHMM
Page 68: © USHMM
Page 71: © USHMM
Page 82: © USHMM
Page 83: © USHMM
Page 85: © USHMM
Page 88: © USHMM
Page 99: @ Ken Setterington
Page 100: @ Ken Setterington
Page 102: @ Ken Setterington
Page 104: @ Gilles Couteau
Page 106: @ Stuart Seeley
Page 108: @ USC Shoah Foundation
Page 110: public domain

Ken Setterington is a storyteller, a children's book reviewer, and a librarian. The author of the ground-breaking picture book *Mom and Mum are Getting Married!*, Ken has been on the award committees for the Newbery, Caldecott and Sibert awards. Ken received the title Librarian of the Year in 2000 from the Ontario Library Association and won the prestigious Toronto Arts Award for Writing and Publishing in 2001. He is a regular book reviewer for CBC Radio and several publications. He has been a storyteller with Queers in Your Ears and has published retellings of *The Snow Queen* and *The Wild Swans*. Ken lives with his partner in Toronto.